GENTLEMEN OF WORTH
HISTORICAL ROMANCE
3

D1527464

A GRAND DECEPTION

*A Gentlemen of
Worth Historical Romance*

Other Books by Shirley Marks

An Agreeable Arrangement
Geek to Chic
His Lordship's Chaperone
Honeymoon Husband
Just Like Jack
Lady Eugenia's Holiday

The Gentlemen of Worth Historical Romance Series:
The Suitor List
Perfectly Flawed

Chapter One

No one knew the real reason Lady Muriel Worth had come to Town. Not her closest friend, Susan Wilbanks, not her Aunt Penny, not even her father, the Duke of Faraday.

However, soon after arriving in London she did confide in Susan. Without her friend's help, Muriel could not have continued with her well-laid plans.

She had come to London to meet a man. A man she had been corresponding with in secret for the last four years. As if that had not been bad enough, she'd managed to slip out from under the protective wing of her aunt to meet him, on more than one occasion. She had only left his company minutes ago and returned to the place where her friend Susan waited.

Muriel slid through the narrow side doorway from the alley into the subscription library. She moved past other patrons who milled about with hushed voices. This gathering, however, felt far less formal than the flirtatious whispering in the crowded ballrooms she'd experienced nearly every evening over the last two months.

"How goes it, Sukey? We have not been discovered, I hope." Muriel exhaled, inspired and exhilarated by her recent meeting. She placed her books on the table with great calm and slid into the seat next to Susan. "I would like to increase my sessions to twice a week."

"You've gone from twice a month to once a week only a fortnight ago. However are you to explain another absence to your aunt, Mrs. Parker?" Susan placed a bookmark between the pages of her novel before closing it. "The subscription library is certainly acceptable once a week for you, but twice? I fear it will not fadge. And my mother would never believe it of me."

Anyone who knew Muriel, the young Muriel, could well imagine her need to go to the library, because at home it was where she spent most of her time. At the age of eleven, Muriel had watched her brother, Frederick, go off to Eton—and learned she could not attend because she had had the misfortune of being born female. She had so wished to learn Latin and then, perhaps, continue on to the Classics. Without a formal education or a tutor furthering her studies, such an endeavor would prove difficult.

The new Lady Muriel's behavior had been carefully fashioned to resemble her elder sister Charlotte's. Pleasant and agreeable, which young Muriel had never been. The new Lady Muriel still appeared to retain some interest in her academic studies but was clearly far more interested in finding a husband.

"I am fortunate you and your mother are staying with us." Muriel drew her reticule close. It contained her notes and the assignments she was to complete. "We have freedoms together I would not normally be allowed if I were alone."

"Mama and Mrs. Parker allowed us to remain at the subscription library unattended while they did some small shopping. We were to *remain,* keeping each other company. Which, you must own, we really have not." Susan removed her gloves from her reticule in preparation to leave. A line of worry creased her brow. "For you spend your time closeted with Signore—"

Muriel shushed her.

Susan fell silent and glanced around them, observing the other patrons to make certain she had not been overheard. "Oh, Moo, if we are ever found out, I fear I should never again be allowed to leave the house."

"Do not worry, Sukey, for you may tell your mother to place the blame entirely in my dish. Aunt Penny certainly will. Do you not understand? This is my first and best opportunity to obtain the level of instruction I crave."

"You have explained your reasoning to my satisfaction, and you have my every sympathy. That is why I agreed to help. I only fear what will happen if you are caught."

How that should happen, Muriel wasn't sure. Had she not taken every precaution to convince her aunt, and her father, that her extreme interest in academics was no more?

She'd spent the good part of a year feigning fascination with what ladies, at her age and position, usually did to occupy themselves. There were unaccountable hours wasted poring over fashion plates, fabrics, and colors while conferring with the dressmakers. Muriel did not even wish to hazard a guess at the time spent choosing new hats and shoes, much less the other worthless gewgaws that, she was told, every fashionable lady needed in her possession.

Just that morning, when Aunt Penny had suggested that Muriel don the decorative puce velvet bonnet instead of her practical straw hat, she had agreed with enthusiasm and without question.

"Tutelage under Signore Biondi means everything to me. I have made progress I never would have achieved without his instruction. I shall do what I must to continue, despite the risk," Muriel stated with staunch determination. "Even if it means pretending I am part of the marriage mart."

"What a hardship, to have suitors fawning over you, dancing with you, and paying court to you," Susan replied in what Muriel considered heavy sarcasm. "Do you not realize that that is exactly what every girl wishes for? And what is it *you* do? Disregard the entire convention. You encourage their attention, only to ignore their interest if it should become serious. How can you turn your back on all your suitors?"

"I am willing to bear what I must to achieve my end. I do value my young men, though. They aid me in my subterfuge. Do not scold me because I have no interest in finding a husband and marrying." Muriel's father had offered his youngest the opportunity to travel to Town for a Season, as he had his two elder daughters. She had accepted. Only her goals differed from her sisters'.

Her father might have thought she was interested in making a match. Muriel thought being in Town was a perfect opportunity to further her studies.

"You don't wish to marry?" Susan's previous sarcasm apparently had fled, to be replaced by astonishment. "Ever?"

"I imagine someday I shall find the notion palatable, but I am fairly confident that that day is very far off." At present, flirting with young men and spending time attracting said gentlemen held very little interest for Muriel. "Have no fear, Sukey. I do not expect you to provide me with an excuse to meet with Signore Biondi for additional sessions. I shall devise other means."

Susan appeared relieved that she would not be included in further deceptive arrangements. It had been difficult, but not impossible, for Muriel to come up with an acceptable plan to slip away from those who would see her chaperoned at every moment.

Muriel's attention shifted toward the front entrance, where a handful of new patrons streamed in. "Here come my aunt and your mother. We shall continue our discussion later, when we are alone."

Once the four returned to Worth House on Hanover Square, Muriel and Susan headed for the cerulean blue parlor to take tea only moments before Aunt Penny's older sister, Mary—Lady Kimball—and her daughter, Constance, dropped by, quite unexpectedly.

"Do not speak of Signore Biondi in front of my cousin," Muriel cautioned Susan, and she quietly took a seat on the blue-and-gold-striped sofa. "Any secret she learns does not remain so for long."

Susan nodded, and Muriel knew her friend would not say a word.

"I must tell you the latest *on dit*." Constance turned breathlessly to face the two young ladies and motioned them near. "Mother and I attended the Wymans' rout last evening. Of course we saw Lord Phipps and Lady Gelsthorpe. Lady Rushworth and her daughter, Lady Harriet, were there. As you know, poor Harriet has been the gossip for the last fortnight because of Lord Gideon's relentless pursuit," Constance told Susan. "But that is not the most exciting news."

"Tell us, Miss Kimball." Susan fairly sat on the edge of

her seat, waiting for Constance to impart the latest tittle-tattle. "I do not think I can wait a moment longer!"

"Do you know who else attended?" Constance took time smoothing her skirts to prolong the suspense. "The new Earl of Amhurst!"

"The *new* earl? What happened to the *old* one?" Susan turned to Muriel, who knew nothing to enlighten her friend, for an answer.

"He died, goose," Constance replied rather curtly. "From what I hear, the new earl is young, tall, handsome, and *eligible.* And he looked upon everyone as if they did not interest him in the least!"

"A picture of perfect *ennui,* eh?" Muriel thought her cousin's enthusiasm a bit much. And to display so much adoration for someone who held those around him in disdain . . . well, she could not help but find a bit of humor in that.

A maid brought in the tea tray, and Constance leaped from her seat.

"Now I must find Mama and be off; we cannot stay for tea. I need to spend extra time preparing for Almack's. It's the first assembly of the Season, and I am sure the Earl will attend. I shall see you two tonight."

"No, I am afraid not, Miss Kimball. I have not procured vouchers," Susan confessed, sounding a bit low because she had been left out. The Almack Patronesses had not deemed her worthy enough to gather with others of the *haute ton.*

"That is a shame, Miss Wilbanks. I'm sure that Muriel will tell you all about him tomorrow." Constance paused at the doorway for a moment before spinning away from sight. "Farewell to you and—*oh!*"

A thunder of misguided footfalls and shrieks told of a near collision in the corridor. Susan's expression mirrored

Muriel's confusion regarding the commotion outside the parlor where they sat.

"I beg your pardon!" a young male's voice cried out in surprise.

"And I beg yours," Constance replied, but she did not sound affronted in the least. "If I did not have to dash home this instant, I would have my cousin Muriel make introductions."

"I fear it is my loss." The gracious bow that must have followed was nearly audible. "I shall look forward to making your acquaintance next we meet, then."

Both half rising from their seats, Muriel and Susan stared at each other, wondering about the identity of the young man. His voice sounded very familiar.

"*À bientôt, monsieur.*" Constance's *adieu* faded with her gradual retreat and ultimate exit from the premises.

The butler directed the visitor with, "The young ladies gather in the blue parlor, sir. I shall introduce you at once."

"No need to bother, Ralston." A few moments later a dark-haired, finely dressed gentleman wandered in.

"Sir Samuel!" Muriel cried, standing upon recognizing him. "How delighted I am to see you."

Susan followed suit and rose to meet him.

He held his hat and walking stick in one hand when he entered, greeting them with a most splendid leg. "I am most pleased to see you again, Lady Muriel." He bowed over her hand. "Your sisters insisted I stop by to pay my regards and catch up with family news."

"*Both* sisters?" Susan remarked. She stepped out from behind Muriel where she could be seen.

"Why, yes, I—" Sir Samuel Pruitt stopped in midsentence and gazed upon Susan as if he had never seen her before.

"You remember my friend Miss Susan Wilbanks, do you not?" Muriel gestured off to her side.

"Oh, yes, of course." Sir Samuel reached out for Susan's proffered hand and bowed over it. "Excuse me for not recognizing you. Last we met, you were merely Miss Susan, but now you have grown into a very lovely Miss Wilbanks."

Susan thanked him for the compliment with a shy smile and a soft blush.

"Leave your hat and stick with Ralston," Muriel bid him. "Aunt Penny would insist. You cannot deprive us of your company now. I insist you stay."

He glanced at the laden tea tray that gave every indication they had yet to pour out. "I have no wish to intrude."

"Nonsense," Muriel cried. She made space for him on the sofa. "You will sit here, between us. We shall learn all your news, and you shall have all of ours."

Sir Samuel agreed to join them. He left the ladies for only a moment to dispose of his *accoutrements* and returned to the parlor.

"Now we may begin." Muriel busied herself with the teacups, pouring a bit of milk into each. "Gusta and her husband just welcomed a daughter six months ago. They named her Sarah."

"After your mother? How nice." Sir Samuel accepted his tea.

"Little Michael is thrilled with his new sister, but then, he is only just two years old. I imagine he'll be delighted with any playmate," Muriel continued. "And Char-Char and Sir Philip are expecting their first child any time now."

"My siblings have not yet reached the age to marry," Sir Samuel informed them. "I do so look forward to the days when my family can celebrate new additions." He smiled at the prospect.

Could he have any inkling of Muriel's true feelings regarding wedded bliss? Muriel wondered. As much as she may have appeared to be entertaining the idea of marriage, she had no intention of taking that step.

"Allow me to come to the primary reason for my call, besides relaying good wishes from your sisters," Sir Samuel began. "You have previously expressed an interest in seeing the bit of Hadrian's Wall that runs through my family's property up north." He was quick to continue before Muriel could speak. "You need not remind me that I have promised to show it to you someday—and I shall. If such things still appeal to you, I thought you might like to see the nearby Roman ruins, since we are both in Town."

"Here? You mean, in London? Would you? Could you?" Muriel tried to curb her enthusiasm and nearly dropped the teapot in her excitement. "Take me there, that is?" She regained her composure and continued in a much calmer fashion. "I still regard such things . . . as interesting, even now."

"If Miss Wilbanks would care to join us"—he glanced in her direction—"I'm certain Mrs. Parker will think our small party should not look at all odd if we were to travel unchaperoned."

"What do you think of Sir Samuel's idea, Sukey?" Muriel held out a cup. She did not believe her friend would disappoint her by refusing.

Susan accepted the teacup, glanced at Sir Samuel, and gave in. "Very well."

Muriel really must do something for her most accommodating friend. "And by the sound of your encounter with my cousin Miss Kimball, only moments ago, she, too, will be delighted to accompany us if we should extend an invitation."

"Excellent! How delightful that your cousin should share

your interest," he remarked. "We shall make a splendid party
of it, then."

Muriel had no objection to her cousin accompanying
them, though she actually thought that Constance would
not find their group's destination as interesting as she would
Sir Samuel's company.

As for Muriel, she could hardly wait. However did she
think it was possible to hide her true self when an exciting
excursion such as this came along?

It was so much easier for Muriel to defer to her abigail,
Lydia, and to Aunt Penny regarding the appropriate wardrobe for Almack's. It was beyond comprehension how two
grown women could fuss over a gown when all that was
suitable for Muriel during her first Season was white. What
a silly to-do they were making. In her wardrobe there were
a dozen white gowns from which to choose—and for Muriel, one was not any different from the next.

Muriel dressed in her gown of white silk. This one was
embossed with small white flowers and boasted a pale green
ruffle at the hem that matched her sash. She made the expected show of excitement, exclaiming, "There could not
have been a finer choice for my first appearance!"

She secretly hoped that her aunt had not seen beneath her
duplicity and observed how truly boring Muriel believed the
whole social scene. The parties went on and on, night after
night. But she endured dancing and the gentlemen's attention, knowing that this would ensure her continuing residence
in Town.

Muriel entered Almack's on the arm of her father. She
stood tall and held her head high. Lady Castlereagh, a Patroness of the establishment and an acquaintance of her father's, had the honor of introducing her to the other guests.

That evening, and it had only begun, Muriel made the acquaintance of more young men than she'd met in the last two weeks. She smiled, charmed to make each of their acquaintances, or so she told them. The introductions seemed to go on forever, and she knew that once they came to an end, she'd be obligated to step out onto the dance floor with many of the gentlemen.

She abhorred dancing and thought it a waste of time. Not that she was ill-equipped . . . on the contrary, both her sisters, Augusta and Charlotte, believed Muriel was quite graceful and made the complex steps look effortless.

Over the last five years, she had suffered through many lessons, prior to Augusta's, then Charlotte's, coming out, with a third round of lessons before her own presentation to the *ton*.

During one of the dance intervals, Constance, who was ever-vigilant to the comings and goings of the guests, alerted her friend Lady Amelia Whipple and Muriel to a noteworthy arrival.

"Mind you do not both turn and gawk at his lordship at the same time, but that is *him,* over there." Constance pointed from behind her fan.

Muriel was the last of the trio to gaze in the indicated direction. *Him,* she supposed, referred to the Earl of Amhurst, whom Constance could not stop talking about.

"He reminds me of the Prince Regent but not so old and not so fat," Lady Amelia said upon seeing the Earl.

"He reminds me of Lord Byron!" Constance mused aloud after further study. "Except much taller."

Muriel turned and regarded this Adonis, thinking he appeared nothing like the Prince Regent nor Lord Byron. He did appear somewhat familiar to her, but she could not say from where.

"Turn away, girls." Constance bodily moved Muriel by the arm. "I believe the Earl looks in our direction."

"How fortunate we are. The Earl of *Ennui* is taking notice of us," Muriel murmured, but not so softly that it escaped her cousin's ears. What a bother these two were making over the man.

"How dare you!" Constance straightened and raised her chin, addressing her cousin in defiance and scolding in a whisper, so as not to be overheard, "Lady Muriel Worth, how could you be so dim? The Earl of Amhurst is the catch of the Season. The circumstance of his ascension to his position has caught the sympathy of the *ton*."

"Sympathy?" Muriel couldn't imagine the self-important high-flyers with whom she'd kept recent company having compassion for anyone.

"You see," Lady Amelia added, "no one knows *who* he really is."

"If he's only just come into the title, then why is he in the petticoat line and not in mourning?" It was clear to Muriel that the others were far more interested in leg-shackling the Earl and not about his proper social conduct.

"Exactly. There are so many unanswered questions regarding who he is. How is it no one knows? He's such a mystery." It seemed Constance was doing all she could to enhance the tale she'd begun that afternoon.

"Do you not wish to know the answers, Lady Muriel?" Lady Amelia appeared anxious to follow Constance's lead. Both were making complete ninnyhammers of themselves.

"I do." Constance's gaze upon the Earl was intense, indeed.

Muriel almost felt sorry for the poor man.

"I cannot wait to discover where he has been keeping himself and what he hopes to accomplish by coming to

Town." Constance might have had a very dull Season, indeed, if there was not someone such as this earl to draw her interest.

"I daresay I believe any of us could attract his attention, but you, Lady Muriel, are the daughter of a duke, and you, Miss Kimball, having a close connection to the Duke's family, must have a better chance to interest him. Lady Muriel"—Lady Amelia turned toward Muriel with her back to the Earl—"I believe his lordship is staring at you."

Muriel turned her head, glancing at Lord Amhurst and quickly averting her eyes when she detected that he had, indeed, been gazing at her. "Is that what he wants? Social connections?"

Earl or no earl, Muriel did not care for his attention. Handsome, rich, or shrouded in secrets, she simply did not care. And she wished he would take notice of some other girl, someone who would be more receptive.

"Oh, come now, Muriel, give him a nice smile. Let him know you are pleased," her cousin encouraged her.

"I will do no such thing. Honestly, Constance." Muriel addressed her cousin a bit more sternly than she ought. Well aware his lordship's attention had not moved from her, she uttered under her breath so softly that neither her cousin nor Lady Amelia could hear, "The only possible way that man could hold my interest would be if he were accomplished in Latin and made the Classics his life's course of study!"

A lull fell over the room before a male's voice rose above the general murmur of guests. "By Gad, is that you, Moo?"

Chapter Two

*M*oo? That Lord Byron look-alike had the audacity to call Muriel *Moo* while in the midst of Almack's? This was an outrage—her childhood name shouted out in public.

Muriel had thought she could never be humiliated for the simple reason that she did not care about the opinion of others. Apparently she had been wrong. Not only was she horrified, but the attention of every person in the large room was now focused upon her.

A fire flaring in her stomach and her cheeks burning, Muriel wanted to scream in frustration. She was quite simply mortified by the man's lack of decorum. How did he even know her? Could it be that he was known to her and she had not recognized him? Who was he that he knew she was called Moo by her family and closest friends?

The Duke of Faraday summoned one of the Almack's Patronesses with a small gesture. Lady Castlereagh was at his side in a thrice.

"Who is that young man?" The Duke's voice was soft yet

commanding, and Lady Castlereagh seemed to wither ever so slightly at his inquiry.

"He is the new Earl of Amhurst, Your Grace," her ladyship said tastefully from behind her splayed fan.

"Ah, yes. I seem to recall hearing that the previous earl passed on. Apparently the new earl cannot sit in the House of Lords." The Duke glanced at Aunt Penny and Muriel. "He has not, as of yet, reached his majority."

That would make him a *very* young peer, indeed, Muriel mused. It might explain the older woman in black crepe and the all-business manner of the gray-haired gentleman with a black armband attending him. Perhaps they were more advisors than companions.

"I would like to make the acquaintance of this Earl of Amhurst, if you please," His Grace replied.

An introduction was not what Muriel wished. She wished the earl in question to take notice of anyone else in the room. Perhaps she could claim to be disgraced by his remark and suggest to her father that they simply leave?

"Of course, Your Grace." Lady Castlereagh stepped away to speak to Lord Amhurst and his entourage regarding introductions and within several minutes led the group toward the Duke and his family.

"His lordship is more than delighted to make your reacquaintance and that of your family, Your Grace," Lady Castlereagh relayed the message.

Reacquaintance? There must be some mistake. Muriel did not know him. Surely she would have remembered their introduction. The Earl inspected her, from her hair down the length of her embossed white silk gown to the toes of her pale green dancing slippers. She dared not meet his gaze, not with him standing next to her.

"Your Grace, may I present the Earl of Amhurst?" As protocol dictated, the Almack's Patroness presented the newcomers to the Duke first.

During the lengthy introductions, Muriel glanced at Lord Amhurst, deciding upon closer examination that there was, indeed, something very familiar about him. His face was not immediately known to her, but his straight brown hair and the questioning set of his eyes . . . There was something there vaguely familiar, and recollection seemed just out of her reach.

Lord Amhurst's returning "How do you do?" was not uttered in a familiar voice. He narrowed his eyes, squinting, as if attempting to put her in focus.

Muriel became quite aware of the other guests around them inching away. It was almost as if she and the Earl were standing in the middle of the dance floor or on a stage completely alone in full observance of the other guests. The feeling of being on display washed over her.

The Earl brought his quizzing glass to his eye. "It *is* you. What are you doing here?" He continued the conversation that had somehow started with his undignified bellow of *Moo* from across the room. "Do you not recognize me?"

No, she did not. Even staring at him, at this proximity, Muriel was no closer to knowing his identity.

He tugged at the edge of his waistcoat and instantly lost his grip on the fabric, as if he were unaccustomed to directing his fingers when they were encased in soft, pliable kid leather.

"It is *I*"—he touched his white-gloved hand to his gold-shot scarlet waistcoat—"Sherwin."

She could only stare at him. Muriel felt the blood drain from her face in shock. Her mouth went completely dry, and she had difficulty finding her voice, or any suitable words she might string together in response.

"Sherwin Lloyd . . ." Aunt Penny remarked, and she also seemed taken aback by his identity. "Imagine, after all these years, the two of you crossing paths again, right here in Town, in the middle of Almack's."

"*Again?* Have they met previously?" The Dowager Countess Amhurst seemed surprised, and her remark might not have been meant in a pleasant way.

Muriel and Sherwin's exchange was kept private by the distance of the people looking on. At least he had the good sense not to raise his voice.

"I thought you were still at Faraday Hall. I never, ever expected to see you here." His original surprise moved to irritation. He spoke in a sharp manner but no louder than a whisper. "I believe that was where your *last* had originated."

"Considering *it* must have traveled from Yorkshire, where it was addressed, to London, I'm surprised you've managed to receive *it* so quickly," Muriel replied, and she allowed a completely false smile to slide across her lips. "If you continue this rant, you shall give the current gossip regarding the mysterious earl a new turn: the mysterious *ogre* earl!"

"Look, the children are reacquainting themselves," Lady Amhurst commented, now seemingly pleased at the reunion.

Muriel drew in a breath to calm herself and noted that the upturn of Sherwin's mouth was not as convincing as her recently well-practiced one. "Your letters mentioned nothing of *you* coming to Town."

"And what about you?" Sherwin's stare hardened. It was an accusation that she had done the unthinkable, charging her with telling an outright lie.

Muriel answered his quiet accusation with silence. This

was not the place where they should be airing the exchange of their private correspondence, no matter what the volume. Not unless they wished the guests, both families, and all of London to learn of it. Before noon tomorrow word would have spread of their illicit communication.

Was this unpleasant, odious young man truly the shy, soft-spoken Sherwin whom Muriel thought she knew? She could not make any sense of what was happening.

This *must* be he. But this man was tall and broad-shouldered, not the small, slender lad she'd met four years before with whom she'd shared her interest in Latin studies, her hopes to continue to Greek literature, and discussions of her precious books. His once-trembling tenor voice had changed to that of a grown man, deep and solemn, and, at this particular moment, very annoyed.

What had happened to him? What of their years of intellectual exchange, their shared admiration for Latin and the Classics?

His mother rapped her fan on his shoulder. "We are leaving at once." She turned to the solicitor, Mr. Gibbons, and ordered, "Call for the carriage."

Without a pause, Lord Amhurst ended his ephemeral conversation with a concise and overly polite, "Perhaps we shall have the good fortune to meet again."

"I believe that is what you said when we parted last." Muriel could not bring herself to smile at him, not even a civil one for the public's behalf.

"The difference is that the last time I spoke them, I sincerely meant those words." His curt bow was followed by his hasty and immediate exit.

He had never meant to shout out her name, especially not *that* name, the one he'd picked up upon hearing her sisters' usage some years ago. He had used it out of a habit of convenience over their subsequent years of correspondence.

Sherwin could not blame Muriel for not recognizing him. It had, after all, been a very long time. He had not known who she was until he'd "overheard" one of her companions refer to her. He'd been honing the skills he'd long ago learned from the Duke of Faraday's youngest daughter. In her missives, she'd given him some helpful techniques on mastering the art of deciphering spoken words from a distance, as he had offered her some aid in her Latin studies.

He retrieved his hat, cape, and silver-topped ebony cane. After setting the hat on his head, he swirled the cape around his shoulders. Sherwin stalked to the front door to wait for his coach. He was tempted to look back but did not wish to risk seeing her or chance meeting her gaze.

He had never expected to see her here in Town. Why hadn't Muriel written of her impending visit? Their reunion might have been more pleasant. But then again, why would she divulge such information to him? Their communications had always been based on learning and academics. They never touched upon personal matters.

So when he learned that his elder brother Charles had died in the war more than seven months ago, Sherwin had not told her.

He thumped his cane on the floor, frustrated with the waiting.

When his eldest brother, James, Viscount Marsdon, had caught the fever and passed from this world to the next four months ago, Sherwin did not write of it.

Two thumps of his cane did not cause his carriage to appear any sooner.

His father had lingered a fortnight after James had passed,

suffering from the same illness. The Earl of Amhurst had followed his eldest son and heir's death, leaving Sherwin the sole male, the new Earl of Amhurst and Viscount Marsdon. As ever, avoiding any personal topics, Sherwin could not in good conscience relay his life-changing, very sad, and deeply personal news to Muriel, so he had not.

Unable to remain under the same roof as Muriel now, Sherwin passed through the front doors to wait outside.

Never had they disclosed any details of their personal lives. Writing to her of his circumstances would have been out of the question. So how could she know what unfortunate events had befallen him and brought him to Town? Not only had his mother insisted, but the solicitor had supported her position that he set aside mourning and attend the Season to find a bride.

The earldom needed an heir.

To be honest, Sherwin found it embarrassing to think of such things.

But Muriel had never hinted that she was interested in going to Town for the Season. For some unconscionable reason, he found it difficult to believe she would ever consider joining the marriage mart.

It was difficult to think of her seeking a husband.

The last he'd seen of her, she'd been thirteen years old and looked every bit a girl, with her simple schoolroom frock and her hair knotted into a bun at the base of her neck. He recalled glancing at her this very night while she stood with her friends. She was tall and slender now, with her brown hair bound on the top of her head. Dark curls framed her face with those wide green eyes, and she had glared at him with complete revulsion.

Yes, he had lied to her. It amounted to as much, in any

case, and it made him feel quite ill. On the other hand, had she not done the same?

Back in the assembly rooms, Muriel was determined not to add to the speculation that was sure to follow the brief, awkward, cryptic conversation she and Sherwin—Lord Amhurst—had had before the guests.

She thought him a horrible, odious man.

The dancing continued, even after Muriel's unladylike display. Many guests were occupied playing cards. The Duke made his excuses and joined his acquaintances in another room, leaving Aunt Penny to chaperone Muriel.

Constance turned to her cousin only moments after the Duke had excused himself. "Whatever was that about?"

Even though her cousin might have been the only one besides the Duke or Aunt Penny in the position to ask that question, Muriel had no wish to answer. She did not wish to explain how matters stood between her and Sherwin Lloyd, now Earl of Amhurst.

Lord Peter, all thoughtfulness and caring, approached Muriel only moments later. "Are you quite all right? He didn't say anything out of line, did he? Need I call him out?"

"Oh, don't be ridiculous, Lord Peter." Muriel did all she could to dissuade him. The very notion that he should challenge the Earl of Amhurst to a duel was absurd, not to mention illegal. "Besides, it's not your place to suggest it."

"How could you say such a thing? You know how much I care for you. . . ." His address was most sincere, and he took up her hand in both of his, staring at her in a most serious fashion, indeed.

She did not care for his behavior. This action convinced Muriel it was time to turn her attention to someone else;

Lord Peter was making a nuisance of himself. To continue her ruse, however, Muriel slid into her more genteel persona. She cast her gaze downward and affected a small, coquettish smile. "Oh, Lord Peter, you most certainly put me to the blush when you say such things."

"You aren't tempted by the Earl, are you?" A glint of fear shone in his eyes. "He hasn't turned your head or—"

Turn her head? Really! Nothing was further from the truth. Muriel wished Lord Peter would stop all talk of the Earl of Amhurst. "Did you not promise me this next dance?" she asked.

It was apparent that he began to see through his cloud of jealousy, and he must have realized that Muriel cared no more for the new earl than she did for yesterday's bread.

They took their places on the dance floor with the other couples and smiled at each other. Our of the corner of her eye, Muriel found herself keeping watch at the door where the Earl had exited, waiting for, and dreading, his return.

"Please do not question me about him." After the dance set with Lord Peter, Muriel once again stood with her family members.

"Why did you not tell us you knew the Earl of Amhurst?" Constance appeared determined to discover why she had not divulged such a thing to her own cousin.

Muriel would not answer and tried to ignore her cousin.

"I will not be put off, Moo," Constance insisted. "You know I will have you answer me sooner or later."

"Oh, very well, come with me." Muriel took a few steps away from Aunt Penny, so as not to be overheard, and she explained, "I did not know he *was* the earl. When I met him, he was a younger son who had no hope of ever coming into his family's title."

How could the shy Sherwin Lloyd, whose passion for education and learning matched her own, have changed into the overbearing autocrat she'd seen tonight?

"But what happened? How is it that he is an earl? Are you not curious?" Constance gripped her fan in what must have been frustration, for Muriel could not and would not answer satisfactorily.

"I do not know, Constance, and I do *not* intend to find out." Muriel did not even wish to think of Sherwin, and she was fairly certain she could successfully forget him if only Lord Peter and Constance would stop bringing up his name. "I have no interest in him whatsoever, and it would suit me well enough if I never had to look upon him and his squinty eyes ever again!"

Would that be enough of a final answer for her cousin?

"Lady Muriel." Sir Samuel Pruitt, dressed in evening finery and knee breeches, an Almack's requirement, appeared at her side and bowed over her hand.

She stepped back in surprise at his sudden appearance and couldn't help but notice Constance's dour expression dissolve with the young man's arrival. Constance's countenance instantly transformed into one of delight.

A spark of recognition flickered in Sir Samuel's eyes. It would be impossible for him to ignore the blinding illumination of Constance's admiration.

"I do not believe we have had a proper introduction." The Baronet extended his right hand to receive Muriel's cousin's outstretched hand.

There would be no avoiding the inevitability of their acquaintance, so Muriel pushed forward. "Sir Samuel, my cousin Miss Constance Kimball."

"How do you do, Miss Kimball?" Sir Samuel replied in all that was proper.

Muriel continued the introduction with reservations. He might decline to claim her as *friend* after growing to know Constance. "Sir Samuel Pruitt."

"I am doing excessively well, Sir Samuel. Thank you for asking." By the glimmer in Constance's eyes and the transformed expression of Sir Samuel's, Muriel began to think she might be wrong.

Oh, no, this could not be. Surely Sir Samuel was merely being polite to return Constance's admiration; he could not truly be taken with her.

No . . .

That was when Muriel learned that, even after the shock she'd had earlier that evening, she could still be surprised.

Chapter Three

The next morning, Muriel rose early, as she had every morning since arriving in Town, and was careful not to make any noise to alert the staff. Lydia had strict instructions not to enter the bedchamber until summoned. Muriel made it a point not to use the bellpull until just before noontime. Everyone thought Muriel spent the early-morning hours sleeping behind the doors of her peaceful bedchamber. Little did they know she spent those hours studying and completing the assignments given to her by Signore Biondi.

Pulling her wrapper tightly around her, Muriel parted the drapes only enough to allow sufficient illumination for her to read and write upon the small table situated near the window. In the time it took to take her pencil in hand and apply it to paper, Muriel's thoughts ran past the scene she had shared with Sherwin Lloyd the night before. She groaned inwardly, scolding herself for drifting off to contemplate what *had* happened, what *should* have happened, and what *might* have happened.

But what a waste of time to think of such things now.

Muriel needed to devise a way to increase the number of her lessons. It seemed unfair that she should spend so much time attending parties and tolerating the attentions of young men and so little time in the classroom.

She would, in time, find a way. The means by which this was to be done hadn't presented itself as of yet. Muriel bent her head to her paper, eager to complete her studies before returning to bed and "waking," the second time, for the day ahead.

Since Sherwin had left Almack's early the evening before, he was fortunate, for once, to have gotten a full night's sleep. He sat at the breakfast table holding *History of Rome* by Titus Livius in one hand and in the other a fork with a bit of gammon and egg from the plate before him.

"I'll have your spectacles now, if you please. It'll soon be time to depart for our morning calls." Lady Amhurst waited for her son to relinquish his most prized possession. "I had not realized you knew the Duke of Faraday's daughter."

"I made her acquaintance some years ago when I accompanied James to Faraday Hall." Sherwin lowered the book to the table and returned the fork, with a bite-sized piece of gammon, to his plate.

"Oh, yes. I do recall that summer. He traveled from Town to Essex after the Season had ended." Lady Amhurst stilled and gazed off somewhere past Sherwin. "James married that fall."

Sherwin had gone back to Eton and missed his brother's wedding. Gingerly, carefully, he removed his spectacles, prying each earpiece from either side of his head, folding the ends, and offered them to his mother.

Lady Amhurst took possession of his glasses. "You and

Lady Muriel appeared . . . familiar, and not entirely pleased to meet the other." His mother was watching him now. "What, exactly, transpired between the two of you?"

"Nothing of importance." He shrugged. "Just some childish larking about. You must remember I had only just turned thirteen when we met—still just a lad." Sherwin was determined to keep the truth from his mother. He knew she would not have approved of his correspondence with Muriel no matter his age.

He pushed around the now-blurry bits of egg and gammon on his plate with his fork. Without his glasses he couldn't see much past the end of his nose clearly. It was his mother's idea that he not wear his spectacles in public. She claimed it would make him appear *bookish,* and no young lady would find that an admirable quality. Sherwin had reluctantly agreed with his mother. He'd agree to almost anything if it meant he could return to his studies.

"I thought her manners were appalling." As always, Lady Amhurst's complaint seemed excessive to his ears. "I'd expect better from the daughter of a duke."

He did not wish to give a name to the unpleasant emotion welling up inside him. No person should harbor such a feeling for another, much less a family member.

"You shall have these again after this afternoon's drive in the Park with Miss Holbrook." With a swish of her black bombazine skirts, Lady Amhurst looked the part of the harbinger of sorrow as well.

"Miss Holbrook," Sherwin repeated, doing his best to commit the name to memory. He would follow all the instructions from his mother to engage the young lady's affections.

"Pay attention, Sherwin, will you?" Lady Amhurst paced along the length of the breakfast room table as she spoke. "I have taken the liberty of sending Miss Holbrook white orchids in your name, if she should mention it."

"White orchids . . . ," Sherwin murmured to himself. His mother knew exactly what to do, and he allowed her to do what she thought was best. He had no interest in courting, much less marrying, anyone. It was best his mother did what was necessary.

"We shall pay a call upon Miss Ortone, Lady Sophie, and Miss Shrope this morning before calling on the Holbrooks, when the two of you will depart for Hyde Park."

Did he need to remember the destination of Hyde Park as well? It was not as if he needed to guide them there. His mother had employed a driver for their carriage to take them wherever they needed to go.

"Don't fret, I'll remind you before our arrival." Lady Amhurst waved her hand as if to tell him to disregard the information altogether. "Now remember, you must compliment Miss Holbrook on her toilette."

Did that mean her hair? Her dress? It was difficult for Sherwin to distinguish much beyond color and general shape, without his spectacles.

"Above all, Sherwin, you must compliment *her.*" Lady Amhurst gestured with his folded wire-rimmed spectacles.

"Yes, Mother." He could certainly do that, and if he did not know what he meant, surely Miss Holbrook would.

"And you should engage her in conversation," his mother continued. "Ask her about herself."

Sherwin highly doubted Miss Holbrook would wish to converse on any topic he found interesting.

"A gel likes to know that a gentleman notices and appreciates the effort she's taken to look her best. It is hours of preparation in front of the glass." Lady Amhurst patted her hair with one hand, then smoothed her skirts as if to illustrate. "We're to attend the Shropes' ball tonight in honor of their daughter."

Sherwin's thoughts drifted to later that afternoon, when he would regain the possession of his spectacles. He could finish the page he'd been reading this morning, if not the entire chapter. Perhaps make it through half the book.

He would broach the topic of allowing him use of the carriage with his mother. There were a few out-of-the-way sights of interest he'd like to visit while in London. His mother might deny him again, but he felt fairly certain she would, in time, grant him his request in order to gain his further co-operation.

"It may take some time, but we shall find one young lady we can mutually decide upon," Lady Amhurst concluded. "To be sure, you shall have a great many to select from. Oh, yes. Do you not know what they call you? The catch of the Season."

Sherwin pulled his gaze from his mother and directed it out the window. Nothing she said would make him care when it came to the choice of his bride.

It was nearly two o'clock in the afternoon before Muriel descended the staircase to the marbled foyer. She had spent several hours preparing for the day, choosing just the right carriage dress and having her hair styled.

"Look at all those lovely flowers!" she exclaimed now, to make it look as if their arrival mattered a great deal to her.

"Place them on the table, if you will," Aunt Penny instructed the footman who carried one small and two fairly large vases of flowers. "We can place them among the others after we've finished our breakfast."

Muriel had to make an enthusiastic show for Aunt Penny's benefit to maintain the illusion that what she wanted, more than anything in the world, was to attend the Season's festivities.

"Sukey, come quickly!" Muriel called up the staircase. "You must see these lovely flowers!"

Susan descended the stairs in haste.

"Are they not beautiful?" Mrs. Wilbanks followed her daughter to the main floor.

"You must help me find Mr. Ambrose's tribute!" Muriel ran around to the far end of the room, making a fuss over finding his flowers. He was the latest young man whom she pretended to favor. There had to be someone, or two or three, for her to feign a slight affection for, else her family might begin to suspect her true agenda of studying Latin and the Classics.

"It seems you are especially taken with that young man," Aunt Penny replied in a knowing manner. She browsed the cards in search of Mr. Ambrose's name.

And that was exactly what Muriel wished her aunt to believe.

"I'm sure they are all for you, in any case." Susan inspected a bunch of violets tied with a white ribbon.

"What a shame that these other gentlemen haven't got a chance of catching your attention." Mrs. Wilbanks joined in the search. "Mr. Ambrose, is it? I thought it was Lord Peter you favored."

"The rest of those gentlemen are all wasting their time," Susan announced. "If only some of them would look my way."

"I'm sure there are more than a few of these posies that belong to you!" Muriel scolded her friend. "Were you not at the Reading rout last night?"

"Well, yes, I was." Susan stilled and stared at Muriel, answering honestly.

"And did you not dance there?" Muriel continued. How could her friend not see herself for the kind, pretty, and most agreeable young lady she was?

"Yes, I did," Susan admitted.

"Were the gentlemen not attentive to you?" Muriel couldn't imagine any male not taking notice of her best friend.

"Why, yes, they were." The color of Susan's cheeks reddened into a deep blush.

"Then there is no reason why any of these could not be for you." Muriel nodded, indicating the collection of pale pink rosebuds. "You see, Sukey? There is no reason to think such lowering thoughts."

"Thank you, dear Muriel. I am glad you can see the right of it." Mrs. Wilbanks wrapped her arm around Muriel in appreciation. "Sukey cannot see how any young man would be interested in her, not while you are around."

"That is nonsense!" Aunt Penny agreed, and she directed her following comments to Susan. "You cannot think yourself in any way unworthy. Your kindness and manners are only second to your grace and beauty."

"You see there, Sukey? I am right!" Muriel chuckled at her friend's foolishness. "Now, let us see who has honored *you* by sending these nice tokens of their affection."

Susan and Muriel searched through the arrangements, identifying the recipient and the senders. Mr. Laurens, Lord Paulson, and Mr. Templeton were found to be a few of Susan's admirers.

"You will let us know if there is someone of particular interest, won't you?" Mrs. Wilbanks leaned between the two young ladies and whispered confidentially.

"Of course, Mother," Susan replied in a guarded manner. "I would never keep such information from you."

"Here they are!" Muriel fawned over the tulips in a tall vase. "Oh, he has outdone himself."

"Do not forget, you and Muriel are to drive in the Park with Mr. Ambrose and Mr. Stanley this afternoon," Aunt Penny reminded them.

"Yes, Mrs. Parker." Susan turned to Muriel to whisper, "I am sure I would not be going if Mr. Ambrose was not in need of a friend for Mr. Stanley."

"Don't be silly, Sukey. Mr. Stanley was quite entranced with you. Could you not tell by the way he watched you that night we met him?" Muriel did not need to pretend on Susan's behalf and merely spoke the truth. "He was rather smitten with the sound of your laughter, if I recall."

"Yes, he was." Susan smiled. "At least that's what he told me."

"Come along, Mrs. Wilbanks, I believe our coffee will grow cold if we dally any longer." Aunt Penny smiled at the young girls and urged Susan's mother down the corridor to the breakfast room.

Muriel beamed a smile so convincing, she nearly thought it genuine and held it until her aunt had well-departed.

Susan turned to address Muriel. "How long do you think you can keep imitating Charlotte?"

"As long as I need." Muriel felt quite satisfied, and the expression on her face must have told as much. "I am rather good at it, if I do say so myself."

"I hate to agree with you, but you do quite a good imitation. I do not understand how Mrs. Parker can believe your playacting, however."

"It is because I am very good at it. Now, the gentlemen will soon arrive, and we must be ready." Muriel stepped away from the flowers. "Let us retrieve our bonnets. I'd hate

Mr. Ambrose to think I did not spend hours agonizing over which he preferred."

"Do you really think he's concerned over that?"

"I believe he is at least as concerned as I am." Muriel opted for the simple straw hat with a riband matching her jonquil dress. "Isn't that always what a proper gentleman's first compliment is to a lady?"

"What a delightful bonnet!" Sherwin handed Miss Holbrook up into the barouche and did his best to appear impressed. It was as close as he could manage to his mother's instructions. "It is quite fetching, indeed."

Lady Amhurst had remained with Miss Holbrook's mother at their residence, and the driver departed with his passengers, the young miss and Sherwin, for Hyde Park.

"Do you really like my bonnet?" Miss Holbrook turned her head to and fro, allowing Sherwin to enjoy an unobstructed view of her headdress. "It is quite fetching, isn't it?"

"Yes, it is very . . . *original*." He studied the ornamentation through his quizzing glass and could honestly say he'd never seen wheat stalks and ribbon used as bonnet trimming before.

The stalks, complete with whole grains, wrapped around the crown, across the wide brim. She might have thought it was a stylish design, but Sherwin had the distinct notion that harvesting might be in order.

"I quite enjoy remaking my headdresses," she began her discourse. What followed were various methods and materials one could employ.

As exhilarating as Miss Holbrook's dialogue had been upon the subject of hats, Sherwin had shifted in his seat until he nearly faced completely away from his companion.

His attention had drifted toward the oncoming traffic. Although he sat some distance away, the occupants in the approaching carriage caught his attention.

It took some time before it occurred to him that he was staring at Muriel . . . Lady Muriel Worth from last night, facing him in a coach. She'd been laughing at first, but all mirth had faded once she'd met his gaze and recognized him.

Since she made no move to respond, he could not, and at this point would not, address her in any fashion. Muriel broke eye contact and moved her gaze away, fixing upon some point ahead in the distance. He followed her example and did the same.

A prolonged silence followed. There seemed to be not a hoofbeat, nor a bird chirping, nor a whisper heard.

"Was that not Lady Muriel?" Miss Holbrook finally broke the quiet.

"I suppose it might have been." Sherwin straightened in his seat and tightened his grip on his walking stick. "By her reaction, or lack thereof, I believe social etiquette does not allow me to acknowledge her publicly."

"I imagine she might treat the gentleman she's out driving with in a similar manner within a day or two," Miss Holbrook lowered her voice to confide in him.

"Why would you say that?" This was the first thing she'd said that had interested him.

"You did not see her bonnet?" Miss Holbrook did not sound as if she cared for it.

Muriel's hat was the least of his concerns. Sherwin would have to confess, if only to himself, that after initially sighting her, he had focused on the two gentlemen seated next to and across from her.

"That was a hat that said, 'It matches my outfit and nothing more. You, sir, are not worth the effort of decoration.'"

"Excuse me?" Had Sherwin heard Miss Holbrook correctly? Muriel did not care for her gentlemen company? And her sentiments were clearly stated by the style of her bonnet? Sherwin did, indeed, have much to learn.

"Oh, no. She does not truly care for *that* man. Mark my words," Miss Holbrook confirmed, and she added a nod of her head for good measure.

Sherwin raised his quizzing glass in earnest, tilted his head back, taking in the entire vision of his companion in all her hat glory, and wondered if her supposition could possibly be true.

"I don't recall that bird on your—" He motioned to his own tall beaver to indicate its position. "It's quite lifelike, I think."

It moved at the exact moment Miss Holbrook cried out in alarm, "Bird? I don't have a bird on my hat!"

"Yes, you do." Sherwin kept a firm hold of the quizzing glass handle and could now see that the feathered creature pecking at the grain was not a mere decoration but a real bird. It was either foraging for a late-afternoon snack or gathering some material for constructing a cozy nest.

Miss Holbrook shrieked, waving her arms in the air out of sheer terror to frighten away the trespasser.

Sherwin pressed back into the squabs, leaning as far away from her as he could manage.

In any case, the bird fled. Park guests in passing vehicles gawked in their direction, open-mouthed and wide-eyed at Miss Holbrook's exhibition. The horses balked, and the barouche lurched forward, nearly sending Sherwin tumbling over the side to the ground.

Chapter Four

I have been informed by her ladyship that you are to wear the dark blue Superfine jacket with the gold-striped waistcoat this evening." Sherwin's valet, Lewis, hung each garment within easy reach.

Sherwin stood in his shirtsleeves and white knee breeches before a full-length pier mirror in his bedchamber. He knew he was little more than a mannequin or puppet for his mother, and not only when it came to dressing. But he simply did not care. Someone had to take charge of family matters. If his mother wanted to assume that role, she was welcome to it.

Lady Amhurst needed his cooperation, however, and Sherwin would do what he must to accommodate his mother. He could not deny he had a duty to the family, no matter how difficult the task.

It was not so much difficult as tiresome.

Lewis spent an inordinate amount of time straightening the fabric of Sherwin's shirt and removing bits of lint. Sherwin stood very still, holding his arms to his sides as not to distract his valet, who reached for a length of linen and wrapped it around Sherwin's neck with precision.

Sherwin hoped for a successful first attempt. It wasn't always so. Sometimes tying the cravat took several tries— and with each attempt the failure was discarded, dropped to the floor, and a new swathe of linen applied.

This whole courting ordeal took up far too much time, as far as he was concerned. If his mother would save him the trouble and simply be so good as to choose a bride for him, he would truly appreciate it.

"I've changed my mind, Lewis." Lady Amhurst strode into Sherwin's bedchamber. "I'd rather he sport a waterfall this evening."

"At once, your ladyship." Lewis' hands froze, then unfolded and unwound the crisp linen he'd been sculpting into an Oriental. He flung it to the side and reached for another to begin again.

Sherwin said nothing, merely endured.

Lady Amhurst moved to examine the waistcoat and jacket. "And not the blue, I think, but the black."

"Yes, my lady," Lewis acknowledged without taking his eyes from his work.

Sherwin remained still, hoping his cooperation would hurry things along.

His mother stepped to the marble-topped bureau where his accessories were laid out for the evening. Two fobs, one for a pocket watch he could not see to discern the time, the other, which hung from his left pocket, simply decorative, and a long gold chain connecting them. He'd also wear a quizzing glass. Not because it helped him to see much, but because his mother considered it a fashionable ornament.

Crafting of the waterfall had been completed. Lewis slipped the waistcoat over Sherwin's sleeves, settling it onto his shoulders and buttoning the front. The quizzing glass went over Sherwin's neck before he shrugged on the jacket, the black one. The valet adjusted the material around the collar, making sure the cravat hadn't lost its shape. He tugged on the cuffs, extending them a half inch from the sleeve.

Lewis stepped back to retrieve the accessories. He placed the pocket watch, gold chain, and fobs in their places, adjusting each to hang at the same length.

"Yes, you'll do nicely," remarked Lady Amhurst, passing her critical gaze over her son. Then she left the room.

"There you are!" Miss Constance Kimball moved to Muriel's side upon sight of her at the Shropes' ball.

"Be aware, Sukey, my cousin approaches," Muriel warned her friend.

"Oh, Moo. It is too bad of you to speak of her so." Susan threw an admonishing glare her way.

"I expect everyone who's anyone will attend the ball tonight," Constance uttered in a confidential tone.

"What is that supposed to mean?" Susan dropped open her fan to cool herself.

"Only that our companion here"—Constance indicated Muriel with the tip of her closed fan—"is the current *on dit,* and they will wish to see what happens next."

Neither Muriel nor Susan said a word.

"You know very well to what I refer, Miss Wilbanks. I heard you were in attendance when it happened. You rode in the very same carriage as Muriel and must have witnessed the entire incident."

"'Incident'?" Susan repeated with her eyebrows raised. "Oh, you must mean the disruption in the Park. It was absolutely ghastly. There was a horrendous shriek that terrified some of the horses, and they bolted, running about, and there might have been a horrible accident."

Muriel clearly remembered hearing Miss Holbrook cry out after she and her party passed the carriage. Why Sherwin cared to be out driving with her was another question. Did he not know she only cared for bonnets and trimmings?

"That's not what I am referring to at all." Constance seemed to ignore the near-disastrous consequence of overwrought passengers, injured equines, and damaged equipage. "The cut direct." She continued, whispering with great urgency. "Our Muriel and the Earl of Amhurst. It was not merely one cutting the other. No, it was quite mutual, so I hear. What do you say to that, cousin?"

Susan glanced from Constance to Muriel.

Muriel already knew what Susan had seen. Nothing. At the time, she'd been occupied in conversation with both Mr. Stanley and Mr. Ambrose. Why couldn't her cousin have inquired about the near accidents? Susan had seen everything that had happened *after* Miss Holbrook screamed.

At the very moment Muriel had caught sight of Sher—the Earl, sitting in a carriage, their gazes had met. She knew without a moment's hesitation that each instantly wished not to have seen the other, and the next moment, for it was only an instant later, slid their gazes away.

Muriel had thought—hoped, really—that no one had noticed. She hadn't glanced around at others in the Park to confirm if she had been correct. It had happened so quickly. How could anyone have seen?

It seemed her assumption was wrong. Evidently those who were present within a twenty-foot radius had borne witness to the deed, and those who lay beyond, but still within Hyde

Park, were then notified by the firsthand observers. Those who resided within the London city limits were then, apparently, informed by secondhand accounts. The remainder of the British kingdom would soon learn of the Duke of Faraday's youngest daughter and the Earl of Amhurst's social slight by post or mention in the gossip columns of tomorrow morning's newspaper.

Ridiculous.

"We need to change the subject." Muriel leaned toward Susan and whispered, then turned toward her cousin. "Have you seen Sir Samuel? There is something I wish to speak to him about."

"Not as of yet," replied Constance. "I shall certainly keep watch for him. He is a most handsome young man. Is there anything you can tell me about him?" The last was said in more than a casual manner.

"Sir Samuel is to be the Duke of Cubberleigh, you know. Someday, that is," Susan informed her. Had she wished to spare Muriel from answering any more questions? "Probably a long time off, for his grandfather holds the title now, and his father, Earl of Hamstead, is next in line."

"Sukey!" Muriel wished her friend would not say so much. Glancing at her cousin, Muriel detected Constance's greedy expression and cautioned her with, "Sir Samuel is as dear to us as my brother, Freddie, or Susan's brother Richard."

"He was hopelessly in love with Gusta, and we all adore him quite as if he were one of our fold," Susan confided in Constance. Muriel thought perhaps that might not have been the wisest action. "He'd make a splendid catch, if only one could gain his attention. It's been four, nearly five years since Gusta refused him."

"I shall set my cap for him," Constance vowed. "If I cannot gain Lord Amhurst's notice, that is."

It was all Muriel could do to hold her tongue. *Think pleasant thoughts,* she repeated to herself. *How would angelic Charlotte behave if she were to face a situation such as this?*

Constance to set her cap for Sir Samuel—what a load of gammon!

Muriel really must rein in her annoyance and not give herself away, or all her planning to attend the London Season would be for naught.

"Lady Muriel." Sir Samuel bent over her hand, looking quite dashing in his evening wear. "I have heard that you wished to see me?"

"Oh, yes." Muriel glanced around, judging if their privacy was adequate enough for their conversation. She slipped her hand into the crook of his arm and urged him to move forward.

"You aren't in trouble, are you?" A worried expression crossed his face. "You know there is nothing I would not do if you—"

"No, it's nothing like that. I do need to ask a great favor of you, though." Muriel stared at Sir Samuel, wondering if she might, if she dared impose upon him.

"You wish me to do something for you, then?" Sir Samuel's expression moved a fraction away from worry.

"Let us stop over there, by the window." They moved to a far corner of the room but not out of sight, where their solitude might look odd. "I need your aid in an endeavor. It might not be an action my aunt or father would approve, but it is a risk I must take. . . ."

"Is it something illegal?" He narrowed his eyes.

"No, of course not. It's nothing of the sort. It is only that . . . I am in need of an alibi, perhaps, and definitely some transportation to relay me to meet with—"

"Not a disreputable scoundrel behind your family's back!" His eyes went wide.

"I wish to meet with my Latin tutor," she said a bit louder than she had intended. A quick glance around told her no one had overheard, however.

"Why do you not simply have him come to the house?" His voice returned to a whisper.

"I cannot. My father will not hear of it. He believes I should not be wasting my time with 'male studies.' He wishes me to spend my time on more genteel pursuits: painting, needlework, or music."

"You have mastered a number of musical instruments, although I cannot vouch for your voice, since I have never heard you sing."

"And you never will," she maintained.

"If I correctly recall, you cannot paint, draw, or create a passable rendition of needlework. So His Grace's words must be falling upon deaf ears. A Latin tutor, eh?" Sir Samuel took his time to consider her words. "How have you come to learn of this *tutor*?"

It occurred to Muriel that Sir Samuel might know her a little too well. "Honestly, Samuel, he had been recommended to me many years ago, and I have been studying with him by post. Now that I am in Town, I have the opportunity to meet with him."

"I see." Sir Samuel not only sounded skeptical, but his expression illustrated as much.

"During Augusta's house party I met Sherwin Lloyd. He came along with his eldest brother, Lord Marsdon. Mr. Lloyd wrote a letter of introduction to Signore Biondi on my behalf." Muriel knew she had to confess everything to Sir Samuel, else she would have no hope of obtaining his assistance.

"Sherwin Lloyd? Isn't he the new Earl of Amhurst I've heard so much about recently?"

"Yes, the very same, I imagine." This was an area in which she did not wish to venture.

"So now you come to London and meet the Earl again." Sir Samuel was sounding more and more like her father or brother than her friend. "From the time you met him last at Faraday Hall, I'm sure he has matured from a boy to a man."

Young scholar to an earl.

"I hardly recognized him." She hadn't at the time. Muriel was unconcerned about the Earl in any case. They were straying from the topic, and she urged Sir Samuel with, "We were speaking of my lessons, if you recall."

"You've been writing to the tutor . . . without your family's knowledge," he repeated, illustrating the significance of her actions by his own rendition of her words. And Muriel was fairly sure he did not approve.

"You must know how important this is to me. Sherwin knew how much my studies meant. He is the only one who has ever encouraged me."

Sir Samuel took more time to reply than Muriel would have expected. A simple yes or no would end her torment. Would he or would he not help her? Why did he not answer?

She must have looked frightfully distraught.

"This may go against my better judgment, but I must know. . . ." A wry smile spread over Sir Samuel's face before he replied, "So, Moo, what is it exactly you wish me to do for you?"

* * *

Sherwin arrived at the Shropes' ball at what his mother considered fashionably late and led the way into the residence with Lady Amhurst and Mr. Gibbons. If it were not for Lady Amhurst's insistence that he mingle, converse, and dance, Sherwin would have made himself much happier by standing in a quiet corner where he would not be disturbed, preferably hidden behind a potted palm or two.

"Our hostess' daughter, Miss Shrope, awaits your escort for the next dance," Lady Amhurst informed her son. "She's the one in the peach confection over in that small group of gels." She nudged Sherwin in their direction.

"I see her." And with his long-sightedness, and without his spectacles, it would be a blessing he would *not* truly see her when he got two or three steps away.

He strode off, crossing the room in her direction, coming to a stop before her, and bowing. Offering Miss Shrope his arm for their dance, Sherwin led her to the dance floor, hearing behind him the stifled giggles of her friends.

The dancers lined up in groups of four couples to dance the quadrille. As Miss Shrope smiled, obviously pleased to be partnered by Sherwin, he did his best not to appear sullen. Standing next to him, Miss Shrope appeared to him an enormous, featureless, peachy-pink blur.

The music began, and the pairs bowed. The couples moved forward and back, around one another with intricate steps, switching sides of their formation. Stepping back to meet his partner to grasp her hand, Sherwin brushed gazes with someone in the last square on the other side of the room.

Muriel.

She stood at a distance where he could clearly see her, as she obviously saw him.

Their momentary lapse in attention caused their partners

to hesitate, and together they blocked the path of the two on-coming couples in their respective squares. The dancing came to an abrupt end as all the couples collided.

Miss Bailey-Davies shrieked, Lord Bradley wailed, and Lady Marianne Wells cried out as all the participants fell to the floor in quick succession, resembling a line of dominos tipping from one end of the room to the other.

Muriel could not help but watch all the dancers go down. It hadn't been her fault, had it? She could not take the entire blame upon herself. Sherwin, the Earl of Amhurst, would need to at least take half. He had been the one to catch her eye, which had caused her to pause in the midst of the dance, which *might have* caused the dancers to collide. And the oaf of an earl had stood immobile, just as she had.

She was glad she hadn't fallen. To be sure, there were nearly a dozen people on the smooth, hard floor. That should have been embarrassing enough, but what she thought worse, or so it seemed, was that she and Sherwin were the only two remaining on their feet. It was quite appalling, really. The two of them remained as if they were the last two pieces on a chessboard.

Which would have made him the king, the victor, and she the queen of the losing opponent. Muriel did not like it, and losing was definitely not a concept that appealed to her.

Following the massive mishap, there were shouts and screams from both the dancers and the observers who filled the ballroom in the moments that followed the cataclysmic tumble. The subsequent attention that focused upon the two remaining upright persons was, blessedly, quickly forgotten, and aid from all quarters rushed to those unfortunate indi-viduals on the floor. Bandages and cold compresses replaced the guests' need for their usual refreshments of punch and biscuits.

Susan Wilbanks' familiar voice, protesting the bump of another dancer that had sent them both to the floor while knocking into other participants, caught Muriel's attention.

"Sukey!" Muriel cried out, seeing her dear friend prostrate next to her partner, Mr. Stanley, who had, upon his fall, expostulated, "The devil!"

Muriel set out at once, stepping over Mr. Ambrose, with whom she had partnered. She carefully moved among the injured—if they were not bodily hurt, then perhaps their status as dancing proficients had been wounded—and made her way to her friend's side.

"Oh, Sukey, give me your hand." Muriel reached down to help her stand.

"I beg your pardon, Lady Muriel. I should have the duty of helping Miss Wilbanks to her feet," Mr. Stanley, who had only managed to sit up, replied.

"It might be best if you were standing on your own feet before you offered to help someone else to get to theirs." Nonetheless, Muriel dutifully released Susan's hand for a moment, though she was anxious to lead her friend out of the way, to somewhere safe from the elbows and knees of the guests who were making their way upright. "Are you hurt?" she asked Sukey.

"I'm quite unharmed—no need to worry, Lady Muriel." Mr. Ambrose arrived at Muriel's elbow, brushing at the sleeves of his jacket.

"I am so gratified to hear that, sir. If you would please be so good as to step aside." Muriel moved in front of him, leaning down once again to help Susan to her feet.

"Ouch!" Susan pulled her hand from Muriel's. "My arm. Oh, it hurts! I must have fallen on it."

"It's not broken, is it?"

"I don't think so." Susan slid her glove toward her wrist to check where she was experiencing the pain.

"Allow me to examine your arm, if you please." Mr. Stanley took hold of Susan's hand, assuming control over her well-being.

"Yes, Stanley's the very man for it." Mr. Ambrose drew Muriel gently back by her shoulders.

"Mr. Stanley knows about broken bones," Susan told Muriel in earnest. "One of his mares broke her leg."

"You are not a horse." Muriel could not tolerate this comparison and scolded softly, "Do not allow him to speak of you in that manner."

"But I do like horses excessively," Susan returned.

"One lovely female is much the same as another, I collect." Mr. Stanley extended her arm in front of her. "Does that cause any pain?"

"N-no, it doesn't." Susan spoke hesitantly, as if expecting to feel discomfort at any moment.

"There, there, steel yourself, young lady." Mr. Stanley prodded her arm gently, starting from her wrist and working to her shoulder.

Susan winced when he touched an area just above her elbow.

"I do beg your pardon." He drew his hand immediately away. "Now, if you will remain still, I need to ascertain . . ." Returning to her arm, Mr. Stanley progressed more slowly around the affected area. "Even though there is no discoloration at present, I believe there is a bit of bruising. There may yet be discoloring in the coming days, but I discern no breakage."

Susan glanced at Muriel upon hearing the encouraging news.

Mr. Stanley completed his examination and announced, "I am pleased to inform you that your arm is decidedly not broken. You are in far better health than my mare, Persephone." He smiled at Susan and winked. "And exceedingly prettier."

Susan blushed, sighed, then gazed up at Mr. Stanley and said, "I do believe that is the nicest thing any gentleman has ever said to me."

It was past one in the afternoon the following day before Muriel descended the staircase. She continued to the breakfast room where Aunt Penny, Mrs. Wilbanks, and Susan sat.

"You can't have slept all this time, can you?" Mrs. Wilbanks gazed into Muriel's face, as only a mother—not hers, but Susan's—could. "Your beautiful green eyes still look as if you could do with a few more hours' rest."

"Let me see." Aunt Penny pushed herself up from the table and moved to the entrance to have a look at Muriel.

"How is your arm this morning, my dear?" Mrs. Wilbanks asked her daughter. "You fell rather hard last night. Might there be a bruise?"

"If there is, I cannot see it." Susan rubbed the affected area. "It does not bother me a bit, Mama. It certainly is a shame that the only time I really had a good look at the new earl was when he stood alone with Muriel after all the other dancers collapsed around him. I must say, the vantage point from the floor was excellent."

Aunt Penny slid her hand under Muriel's chin to tilt her head in order to examine her face. "Your eyes are red, and you do look fatigued."

Muriel blinked. Eye fatigue was a small sacrifice compared to what she'd have to endure the remainder of the day.

"We are fortunate we have no commitments this evening. You may be excused early, since we remain at home for only a family dinner." Aunt Penny drew a chair out for Muriel. "I shall fetch you something to eat. Do you realize we've been out every night for nearly a fortnight?"

"La, Aunt Penny, it will be a relief to stay at home to rest," Muriel affected in a cool tone, lowering herself into the proffered chair.

"There *are* this afternoon's activities. Lord Peter is to take you for a drive at three, is he not? Mr. Ambrose is most put out that you cannot accompany him."

"He has accompanied Moo many times—he has no cause to complain," Susan, who sat next to her mother, replied.

"Shall I resort to strolling around our back terrace with each gentleman as our dear Char-Char did two years ago?" Muriel took this time to glance down at her clasped hands folded in her lap and blink up through her lashes, which is what her dear sister Charlotte would have done.

"It may come to that, I fear." Aunt Penny set a plate of toast and eggs before Muriel.

"I cannot claim to have nearly the number of suitors Char-Char did." She leaned against the back of the chair. "And what problems that caused!"

"Mr. Ambrose has no claim on you; he must wait for another day," Aunt Penny decreed. "I think it would not take much to bring him up to scratch. Although Lord Peter may be on the verge of making an offer."

This was not what Muriel wanted to hear. She had no intention of listening to a proposal from Lord Peter *or* Mr. Ambrose. Her recent decision to move her attention from both gentlemen was proving to be a sound one.

Muriel would insist this afternoon's outing be her last with Lord Peter.

Sherwin had a quick bite to eat before being rushed back to his bedchamber to dress for that morning's round of calls. His mother expected he would take Miss or Lady Whoever for a pleasant drive. He wasn't feeling very pleasant, and he didn't expect he'd be fit company for anyone.

"I wasn't the only one who noticed you were one of the few who did not fall during the quadrille catastrophe. Did you have anything to do with that tragedy last night?" Lady Amhurst hadn't been pleased with the mishap on the dance floor and had groused about it all the way home. She was complaining still. "Pray, tell me no."

"I do not believe so, Mother." Sherwin couldn't imagine how he could have been involved. Although it did seem as if all the guests around him had participated in a human version of tenpins.

"That's a relief. I had heard from Lady Shrope that there was an inexperienced oaf on the dance floor, though she did not tell me of which sex. I am gratified she had not referred to you." Lady Amhurst began to circle him, taking in his appearance. "I believe Lord and Lady Torrington's daughter is someone we should consider noteworthy. We shall call on them first this morning."

"Of course, Mother," was Sherwin's immediate response.

"And since you have cooperated so well, I shall see you are amply rewarded." Lady Amhurst seemed almost giddy. "Tomorrow morning, very early tomorrow morning, before you could possibly be seen by anyone, you may have use of the barouche to visit a pile of ruins of your choice."

"Truly?" His head came up, and he straightened in elation, causing Lewis to tug on the nearly complete cravat.

"Oh, sir—I beg your pardon!" the valet cried. "We must begin again."

Sherwin didn't care. "Thank you, Mother." He felt particularly jolly, which made it possible to endure the torture of one hundred cravats!

Chapter Five

Muriel settled herself on the bench of the modest green curricle while the liveried groom held the horses in place, and she watched Lord Peter climb in and take the seat next to her.

"Hatchards, you say?" Muriel blinked up at him, surprised that he should know she'd like to visit the bookstore above all things. And to think she was near to ending her association with him. Well, even though Lord Peter was providing her with this excellent opportunity, she could not allow a mere visit to a bookstore to sway her mind.

This really was too kind of him, but she had already decided not to see him again.

"I thought you might like to stop there after our drive. Your father told me you were most anxious to see the establishment." After a reassuring tug to his gloves, Lord Peter took up his whip and the ribbons, then with a nod ordered the groom to release hold of the horses.

"You spoke to my father?" The news worried Muriel.

"W-why w-would you do such a thing?" She knew exactly why a young man spoke to a young lady's father. And the prospect was too horrible to contemplate.

Was it too late? Would he propose soon? Surely not in Hatchards bookstore!

"Rest assured, he advised I proceed with caution." Lord Peter smiled, looking to be a bit nervous himself. "His Grace reassured me my position with you remains unchanged."

She pasted on the best smile she could manage and nodded. That was true enough.

The horses sprang forward, and the green curricle moved off. Muriel would need to endure another expedition through Hyde Park before her dream of stopping at 173 Piccadilly, Hatchards Bookstore, came true.

Lord Peter escorted Muriel inside the establishment, and she gazed around, lifting her chin to stare up into every corner of the small room. They moved farther, passing into a second room. Never had she been in the presence of so many books. Bookcases lined the walls and surrounded her as far as she could see.

Books, so many lovely books.

Not even Faraday Hall possessed so many volumes. She dared not express her true feeling, lest she make a spectacle of herself.

"I hear there are six floors." Her suggestion that they should move up the spiral staircase to see them all was put as politely as she could manage. "We have come all this way, after all."

"You are right, of course." Lord Peter placed a protective gloved hand over Muriel's, resting in the crook of his elbow, and guided her past the large counter.

Never had Muriel wished for a different hat, one with a larger brim so she could more easily hide her browsing. She tried her best to read the titles as she walked past, showing as little interest as she could.

"Will you excuse me, please? I wish to inquire about a slim volume of poetry." Lord Peter pointed at a shelf off to his right. "I think you might fancy it."

Poetry? Muriel thought not but answered with a smile, "By all means, do see if you can find it." She pulled her hand from his arm and urged him to move away. "Take as long as you like. I'll just do a bit of perusing myself."

She turned to the bookcase to her left the moment Lord Peter stepped away, and the rich gold decorative scrolling and lettering on the spine captured her attention. *Cursus Publicus: Roads of the Roman Empire.*

Muriel pulled the heavy book from the shelf and pried it open to look inside. Color illustrations covered the large pages, illuminating major ports, roads, and settlements. She ached to spend hours studying each page and admiring the many images. Closing the book, she wrapped her arms around its covers, holding it tightly against her.

Muriel wished to purchase the book, but if her aunt or father learned of it, they would know she had not given up her bluestocking ways. She could not take the risk of discovery.

Glancing at the tome in her arms, then to Lord Peter, who held the small book of poetry in his hands, Muriel thought better of her actions and slid the volume back into place on the shelf.

Her final decision was that purchasing the book would be best left for another day.

That evening was, indeed, quiet. After the weeks of non-stop parties and early-morning studies, it had felt good to stay at home for a change. It had been just Muriel, her father, her aunt, and Sir Samuel for dinner. Then Aunt Penny had to ruin the evening by presenting an invitation.

"The Duchess of Devonshire does not wish to see a repeat of last Thursday's tragedy at the Shropes' ball. Therefore she is hosting a morning practice dance to be held tomorrow," Aunt Penny paraphrased for their benefit.

"But, Aunt Penny, we have only just finished dance lessons with Monsieur Dubois. Do you not think . . ." Muriel had already endured sessions twice a week with a dance master, months before their arrival in Town; it was beyond enough. Not to mention her participation, years earlier, when her sisters needed to prepare for their entrances into Society.

"You cannot deny that you, too, nearly fell," Aunt Penny reminded her. "How you managed not to join the others on the floor, I don't know."

Muriel *had* managed to avoid the massive accident. Her good fortune had been due to her looking at Lord Amhurst instead of joining hands with her partner. "And what of our morning callers?"

The Duke said nothing but motioned to his sister-in-law, whom he must have thought knew better than he.

"I imagine most of the young men will be in attendance. It's the quadrille, dear," Aunt Penny continued. "Obviously, there are young ladies and gentlemen who are having difficulty with the intricate steps."

How was Muriel to plan her escape for her lessons if she were to attend early-morning dancing lessons?

"I do not think you should decline the invitation," the Duke added.

"Of course you are right, Papa." Muriel gave them her best smile.

Because dining that evening had been informal, *en famille,* the Duke and Aunt Penny left the table to retreat to the small parlor where all of them would spend the remainder of the evening. Sir Samuel remained behind with Muriel and called out to her.

"Lady Muriel, a private word with you, please, before we join His Grace and Mrs. Parker."

"Of course, let us step into the breakfast room." Muriel led the way.

"Where are Susan and her mother this evening? I expected to see them here." Sir Samuel walked with Muriel very slowly down the corridor.

"Mrs. Wilbanks and Susan are dining with friends of their family," Muriel told him. "What have you been up to today?"

"I've been busy. Took Lady Embleton's daughter Flora for a drive through the Park this afternoon." Once they stepped inside the cozy room, Sir Samuel eased into a chair.

"You are actually courting someone?" Muriel gasped in disbelief.

"As you are well aware, I still search for my wife. I have for several years now."

"But to marry outside of my family . . ." Muriel settled into the chair next to him. "Papa had his heart set on calling you *son*."

"Unless you own to a fourth sister of whom I am unaware, or you care to engage my affections yourself, I highly doubt His Grace will have his wishes met. I have called upon your cousin Miss Kimball. Perhaps we shall find success in that quarter."

"Never say so!" The sharp reply came before she could restrain herself. Constance and Sir Samuel would never suit. Muriel cast her gaze down, a little embarrassed at her outburst, and softened her tone. "You do what you think is best."

Of course Muriel knew that Sir Samuel wanted to marry. It had been many years since he'd declared himself and proposed to her sister Augusta, and he still hadn't found his future duchess. Sir Samuel was waiting for the right one. The lady he would eventually choose would be a very special person indeed.

"If you think *I* am difficult to please, I fear it will take no less than a Roman god to gain *your* notice," he said with a nod of his head.

Perhaps . . .

Muriel never thought along the lines of matrimony and the type of gentleman she cared for . . . but a Roman god . . . If he were truly Roman, she might consider his suit.

Leaning on his arm, Sir Samuel closed their distance to whisper, "I have been considering your request of the other night."

And? She widened her eyes, keeping silent, waiting for his answer.

"What you plan is not to be undertaken lightly. If we are discovered, your father will make quite sure that my presence no longer darkens your family's doorway. Or he will surely call me out to gain satisfaction if I had any part in your dishonor. I cannot tell you how dear you and your sisters have become—it is as if you are my own family."

My, he had given this quite a bit of thought.

"It could disgrace us and cause a scandal for both our families. And I would deeply regret that above all things."

Muriel had not taken quite such serious consequences into account when she asked him to aid her.

"I cannot imagine how I allowed you to talk me into such a scheme."

Did that mean Sir Samuel would help her?

"It's not half as perilous as you make out. We shall leave

early in the morning and return before I call for my maid after noon." There really was no chance of discovery. Muriel continued breezily. "The staff, as well as Aunt Penny and Papa, understand and accept my fatigue after dancing all night."

"Yes, you do participate in every dance, but you do not fool me one bit." Sir Samuel placed his hands on the arms of the chair and pushed himself to his feet.

"But I do manage to fool them." Muriel could not allow Sir Samuel to talk her out of her plan. Furthering her education far outweighed attending silly dancing parties.

"If I do not aid you, then I am certain you shall find another who will," he said with some resignation. Indeed, Sir Samuel knew Muriel better than she had suspected. He sounded sage as he proceeded with caution. "The only way I will know you are not in harm's reach is if I am the one who makes the arrangements."

Sir Samuel *was* going to help her!

"This is a map to my aunt's town house just around the corner. I've added a few descriptions to help you find the place." He handed her a folded piece of paper with his left hand and dug into a vest pocket with his right. "This is the key to the garden gate. You may let yourself in and wait for me there when it is time."

"Where's your aunt? Isn't she at home?" Muriel eyed the well-worn key and placed it on the crisp, folded paper.

"For these last few years she's closed the town house for the summer and visits her sister in Somerset."

"Very well. I shall put this to good use." Muriel eyed the small metal key, turning it over in her hand.

"It shall make me feel better knowing you're in a safe place and not standing in the street like a hawker."

"Sir Samuel, you are wonderful!" She wanted to leap out of her chair and throw her arms around him but could not risk the undue attention it would cause. "I cannot tell you how relieved I am."

"Lord knows what will happen if we are discovered." Sir Samuel exhaled, clearly concerned over the path on which they were to embark. "If we are forced to marry because I have compromised you . . ."

"Never fear, I shall make you an excellent wife if that comes to pass." She gave him a teasing smile.

"Allow me to reiterate my intention to wed a young lady of my own choosing." He gazed at her with all that was serious.

Muriel made a moue. "I should not tease you, should I?"

"No, you should not." He cleared his throat. "When will you meet with Signore Biondi next?"

"I'll send word for us to meet tomorrow morning. We shall leave early, when no one is about and more than half the town is still abed." Muriel felt quite confident they would not be discovered.

"But what of the Lady Devonshire's party? Mrs. Parker will not allow you to refuse."

"I plan to attend. You'll be astonished how happy I will be to do so." Muriel tended to feel elated after attending her sessions with Signore Biondi. "However, I might caution you that we not be overly friendly at Lady Devonshire's party. Lest we are overheard or give ourselves away."

"That might be best," he acceded with a slow nod of his head.

"Now, let us join the others, Sir Samuel, and pretend we have not just cast ourselves into the briars."

If only Sherwin did not need to attend a party every night. His life was becoming tiresome, indeed. The evenings of leisure reading were gone, and he wasn't sure he'd see them again for a very long time.

This ball, soiree, rout—whatever they called this type of gathering—he spent dancing and "in conversation" with various young ladies.

"What a disaster!" Miss Torrington proclaimed for the fifth time in the scant ten-minute interval she and Sherwin had stood together. "Do you not think so?"

Sherwin inhaled before making a noncommittal reply but did not have the chance to utter an answer before Miss Torrington continued. "I wonder who started it? I'm sure it was some caper-witted gudgeon. Don't you think?"

Sherwin wasn't sure how he'd—

"Do you not know, my lord? Were you not present when it happened? Not watching from the side but among the dancers themselves, I daresay."

If he had to listen to another person speak of the mishap from the previous evening, Sherwin would . . . He wasn't quite sure what would happen, but he felt certain it would be nothing less than scandalous.

"Have I complimented you on your gown this evening?" He offered up one of the standard compliments his mother had given him to use on an occasion such as this. He could not say why young ladies seemed to take his remarks to heart and go on and on about the pains they had endured to achieve their appearance.

"Why, no, you have not." Miss Torrington lowered her gaze. "I thank you for taking notice."

He hadn't noticed anything. Sherwin could not make out any details of her gown, only that it was pale in color—white, if he had to guess. And he prayed that she would not ask if any accessory she wore matched her eyes. He could not distinguish their color.

"It takes some talent to make allowable alterations to a

'white gown,' because you must know that every young lady must wear white during her first Season, but they can be so dull, don't you think?" Miss Torrington continued. "The changes must be very subtle: a soft flourish here, a small, pale ruffle there, a bit of trimming to embellish one's hem or draw attention to one's neckline."

And men were supposed to notice these things?

"A young lady attending her first Season must compete with other young ladies out for their second or third Season who wear colors that are much more expressive. Just as gentlemen have the distinct advantage of wearing various patterns and prints on their jackets and waistcoats."

Sherwin's hands moved to the cloth-covered buttons of his jacket, but the two appendages alone could not prevent her from turning her scrutinizing eye toward him.

"As for you . . ." Miss Torrington tilted her head in his direction. "Your lordship is a very practical man, I'd say. You have minimal but tasteful accessories. The bold pattern of your waistcoat and deep color of your jacket show maturity. They are the work of a fine tailor. Your cravat was obviously sculpted by a competent valet." She smiled, seemingly pleased with him. "You, Lord Amhurst, are one finely dressed, very serious gentleman."

Miss Torrington could assess his character by what he wore?

Sherwin tugged his cravat, which felt as if it was constricting his neck. Then he glanced to the other gentlemen in a halfhearted attempt to assess their appearance as Miss Torrington had his, but he could not see them clearly.

His mother had shopped, chosen, and purchased every item he wore. The "maturity" of which Miss Torrington spoke was his mother's, not his. Lady Amhurst had always taken exceptional pains with his appearance. She must have known exactly what she was doing and what image she wanted him to present.

His companion's observation made him very uncomfortable. Sherwin had no notion that he had been on display while he attended these functions.

The idea of it did not appeal to him at all.

Sir Samuel bid Muriel farewell after their tête-à-tête. He had plans to attend a musical soiree that evening. Muriel then retreated into the small parlor with her aunt, where she did not remain long. Aunt Penny advised her niece that she should be off to bed and acquire the sleep she so sorely lacked.

Upon entering her bedchamber, Muriel found Lydia laying out a night rail and wrapper, preparations for the night.

Lydia turned toward the door. "Is there something you need, Lady Muriel?"

"I believe I am ready to retire for the evening," Muriel informed her abigail.

"It's still very early." But Lydia hurried to close the bedchamber door.

"Aunt Penny bid me to do so, and I must confess, I have been excessively fatigued of late." Muriel stood with her back toward Lydia, ready to be divested of her frock. "I believe my aunt is right: the extra rest shall do me good."

"She and Mrs. Wilbanks have been concerned that you might be attending too many parties." Lydia unfastened the tapes, removed the garment, and laid it over a chair. She retrieved the night rail and slipped it over Muriel's head, allowing it to hang free. "I confess, I might have to agree with her."

"I hate to overly worry her about such things." Muriel sat at her dressing table. "I think an early night will be just the thing to set me to rights."

Lydia agreed. The abigail stood behind her and brushed her long, dark hair and asked about Muriel's beaus and whom she favored and if she thought he might come up to scratch. She inquired after Miss Wilbanks' suitors as well, saying, "Oh, that Mr. Stanley is a great favorite of hers, is he not? And so handsome too."

Muriel made a noncommittal reply.

Muriel's braided hair lay upon her shoulder. Lydia helped Muriel into bed, pulled the covers around her chin, and bid her a good night's sleep.

"Remember, Lydia, I plan to sleep until well after noon." Muriel was sure to remind her. "I shall ring for you when I wake."

Muriel may have gone to bed early, but she was far from falling asleep. She lay still, but her mind was busy pondering the tasks ahead of her. She needed to retrieve the dress, bonnet, shoes, and plain, serviceable cloak she'd hidden. There were notes, paper, pencils, and books already secured in her satchel, which she did not wish to forget. All would need to be placed somewhere quickly accessible so she should not fumble about in the dark early in the morning.

After waiting a good half hour, she drew the covers away, swung her legs over the edge of the bed, slid to the floor, and went to work. She needed to make her preparations to leave down the back stairs and out a side door early the next morning. Above all it was important she keep very quiet.

Chapter Six

As she had planned the night before, Muriel readied herself for travel, donning her plain bonnet and cloak just after sunrise the next morning. Under her arm she carried the satchel containing her notes, extra paper, pencils, and books she would need.

Slipping out of Worth House, she followed the few handwritten directions on Sir Samuel's map. His aunt's town house was not far, well within walking distance. Soon, Muriel stopped before an ivy-covered portal and used the key he'd given her. Pushing open the large iron gate, she stepped inside, off the main street, and latched it behind her.

The dim morning light hardly illuminated the garden. From what she could tell, it looked like a veritable jungle. Not five minutes had passed before a small black carriage rolled to a stop in the street. It was Sir Samuel, come to relay her to Signore Biondi's.

With the aid of the Baronet, Muriel entered the vehicle and settled on the bench seat across from Sir Samuel.

"Let us be off." Sir Samuel glared at her from his side of

the interior. With a quick double tap to the roof, the carriage sprang into motion. "This is most improper, Muriel. I cannot see how His Grace could condone our actions."

"I'm not asking for his blessing." Muriel placed her satchel next to her. "I trust you implicitly. I know you shan't allow any harm to come to me, chaperoned or not."

"That is quite true. Would it be wiser to have your brother, Freddie—"

"No." Muriel didn't expect Sir Samuel to understand. "He and Papa are thick as thieves and cannot be trusted. You are the only one whom I can depend upon."

It was clear Sir Samuel was not particularly pleased with her—further proof he might as well have been her brother. If not by blood, then she would claim their relation stemmed from their mutually disagreeable opinions.

For most of the hour during her session, Signore Biondi sat behind his massive, ornately carved wooden desk. Muriel would not have been surprised to discover it originated from the time of the Italian Renaissance. He kept his head lowered, focused on a pad of paper before him. She might have suspected he was ignoring her except for the few times he raised his index finger and corrected her pronunciation.

Muriel was then obliged to stop and repeat the phrase. A rustle of movement coming from the doorway distracted her.

"*Si,* Giorgio, *grazie.*" The Latin tutor glanced over his narrow, wire-rimmed glasses, acknowledging the intruder with a nod.

Muriel finished reading the last sentence aloud and then faced her tutor.

He did not look up but kept working a pencil. Had Signore Biondi been taking notes? Had he been making so many comments on her errors today, it took him much longer to finish writing them out?

"Enough, *Signorina*. Well done." He set whatever he'd been working on aside and removed his glasses. "We shall continue next time we meet. I believe your young man has arrived to see you home."

"Thank you, *Signore*." Muriel closed her book and collected the papers before her. She stood and stepped out of the room. Continuing down the short hallway toward the front door where Sir Samuel waited, Muriel retrieved her cloak and bonnet.

"A successful session, I trust?" Sir Samuel greeted her.

"Yes, very." Muriel pulled on her bonnet and tied the ribbons. "I thank you for returning for me."

"I couldn't very well leave you to find your own way home." He swung his beaver hat onto his head by the brim and stood ready to depart at the doorway.

They stepped outside the modest apartment, one in a row of buildings, as it neared noon. Muriel needed to get home and crawl back into bed.

Sir Samuel took her hand to help her up the steps of his carriage. He entered after her and sat on the opposite bench. The steps were folded up, and the door closed behind them.

The vehicle moved forward, and Muriel could not keep a smile from touching her lips. "It was wonderful. I do not know how I am ever to repay you."

"You could forget this madness and be satisfied, as any other young lady, to attend the endless round of parties," he suggested without humor. "I'm quite certain that if you could form an attachment, it would delight your family to no end."

"Oh, no. I cannot do that." Muriel pulled her satchel closer, wrapping her arms around it tightly. Did Sir Samuel think he could change her mind? "Even you must own that I am not any ordinary young lady."

"I'm afraid you are correct, there." He pushed his hat to the back of his head and sighed, making him appear quite exasperated. "And I fear for Mrs. Parker and His Grace, for they are involved in a battle they cannot win."

"You make it sound as if I am a spoiled child who must have her way."

"Willful, impulsive, perhaps, but not spoiled," Sir Samuel clarified. He cleared his throat. "I find you also inquisitive and intelligent, which would not be considered a compliment to any fashionable young lady. I should receive a resounding scolding for speaking my mind, as should you."

"How amusing you are—what was that?" Muriel spied what she thought was a crumbling wall from the window. "Stop the carriage! Stop, I say!"

"What is it? Is something wrong?" Sir Samuel cried out in alarm.

The momentum of the coach began to slow, and Muriel leaped out the door before the vehicle rolled to a complete halt.

"No, look! Isn't it beautiful?" She ran toward the crumbling archway without a worry about its stability. A strand of hair escaped from under her bonnet and blew across her face; she continued without attempting to brush it aside. Once inside the structure, she stopped in her tracks. There, standing before her was the Earl of . . . no.

It was Sherwin. His dark hair tousled, and wearing his wire-rimmed spectacles, he'd been examining some inscription on the wall. She'd startled him, and he turned at her sudden entrance.

They stood there for what felt like an eternity, staring at each other. Motionless. Speechless. Breathless.

"I beg your pardon, Lady Muriel," he whispered. His voice sounded deeper than usual, as if laced in sleep. Then he bowed before departing as suddenly as she had arrived.

Muriel stood amid the ruins alone. She never would have thought he would be here. If she had given it some thought, of course this was a place he would wish to visit, just as she did. But why now? Why had he been here just as she arrived? The chances of them arriving at the same place at the same time . . . it seemed too much of a coincidence.

Yet he could not have known she would be here. And Muriel had had no idea of Sherwin's presence before she arrived. Clearly they were alike, still very much alike, in so many ways. She supposed he truly hadn't changed that much.

No, he hadn't.

And hadn't he looked more like himself, his old self, the one Muriel remembered, when he wore his spectacles? She preferred him that way, studious and handsome. How she wished he could have remained to inspect and study the ancient walls with her. She would have so liked to have his company.

"Lady Muriel?" Sir Samuel entered from the same portal as she had. "Is there anything amiss? I saw someone running out."

"No, everything is fine." But it wasn't. Muriel's reason for visiting the site seemed to dissolve like the crumbling walls around her.

Somehow her discovery of this Roman wall wasn't as momentous as she'd first thought, once she'd realized that the opportunity of sharing it with someone who would enjoy it with her seemed more important.

Sherwin returned home in ample time to dress for the Devonshire dance practice. He now stood in the middle of his bedchamber with Lewis, going through his usual dressing ritual.

A green vest hung next to his Egyptian brown jacket, his mother's choice for this morning's gathering.

"I wish to wear the light-blue-and-white-striped silk waistcoat, Lewis." Sherwin felt the colors of the clouds and clear blue sky better suited his mood. The words had tumbled out of his mouth. What his mother might think about his voicing an opinion regarding his clothing, he wasn't certain. Making his own preferences known to his valet was tantamount to countermanding Lady Amhurst's orders.

Lewis stilled, standing motionless for several moments. For the first time Sherwin noticed that the valet had been taken aback.

"Her ladyship instructed me that you should don the green brocade," he replied in unsteady tones. "She was very insistent that you should look especially your best for this morning."

"Of course." On the whole, Sherwin had no complaints. "That's fine. Proceed." He held out his arms, allowing the valet to slip on the green vest and settle it onto his shoulders before fastening the buttons at his midsection.

His morning had started out wonderfully. Sherwin had risen early, as his mother instructed, and left the house before the rest of London woke. At that time of the morning, his barouche had rolled along the deserted streets alone. He knew where the Roman wall was located but had had no idea how to get there. Actually, Sherwin found getting around anywhere an overwhelming task.

At Eton, if it were not for the other students he could follow, he would be at a loss as to his direction. The city was no better. Sherwin was continually confused as to how he had arrived at a certain place, and he had no idea how to return from where he had come. It had always been so for him.

To make getting about worse, he did not know how to ride a horse, nor did he know how to drive a pair; thus his need for a coachman.

After Sherwin had arrived at the Roman wall, his visit had been cut short, which hadn't pleased him. Running into Muriel had been completely unexpected.

In that moment they'd met in the ruin, he remembered exactly what had drawn them together: her inquisitive nature and their mutual thirst for knowledge. It had been similar to the first time they'd met. She had discovered him in her favorite chair reading her copy of Publius Vergilius Maro's *Aeneid*. At first Muriel had been furious that he dared touch her books, but then, when she'd realized he was reading the untranslated version, respect had replaced her anger. They had been friends ever since.

Muriel's appearance that morning had startled him, but her reaction upon seeing him had taken him completely by surprise. She had softened toward him somewhat, perhaps hating him a little less.

The sentiment had been reflected in the brief smile and sparkle in her eyes that was evident even to him. Sherwin suspected that she was unaware of the change in her own feelings, but he had to admit that he was pleased.

He could well imagine that her interest in the crumbling wall was the same as his. But what was she doing there at that hour in the morning?

After he had excused himself and left her company, he'd dallied just outside. He hadn't thought he'd reenter, but he could not quite bring himself to depart. That was before he saw a man, a young man, follow her inside.

The site had not been preserved but merely remained and,

most likely, was not often visited. Sherwin was certain it hadn't meant much to most people except for him and . . . perhaps Muriel.

The appearance of her companion had given Sherwin ample reason to return to his carriage. Leaving the premises, he had passed their empty, closed carriage. Despite his ineptitude in all things social, even Sherwin knew the impropriety of an unchaperoned couple using such a vehicle and could not imagine that the Duke or Muriel's aunt Mrs. Parker would have approved.

Something was not quite right.

His mind was a jumble. He could not erase the memory of their chance encounter, nor could he prevent the moment of their meeting from repeating itself in his mind.

"You are dressed, my lord," Lewis announced. "I hope you are pleased."

Sherwin stepped back from the full-length glass to where he could clearly see himself.

The color of his waistcoat stood out in contrast with the brown of the jacket and the fawn of his knee breeches. He narrowed his eyes in consideration. It was then he realized he didn't care for green.

Muriel and her aunt entered Devonshire House after one in the afternoon with a number of others. This gathering was more informal than a ball.

Aunt Penny faced Muriel to unfasten her niece's cloak. "Your eyes," her aunt whispered on a sigh. "You look no more rested than yesterday. I insist you march straight to your bedchamber once we return."

"Have you forgotten? Sukey and I are to drive out with Mr. Ambrose and Mr. Stanley. They have promised us something very special!"

"Oh, yes. How will you ever catch up on your rest?" Lines of worry appeared upon Aunt Penny's forehead. "When did your constitution become so delicate? I always remember you as a healthy, robust child."

"I cannot say, Aunt Penny." Muriel thought perhaps she might make some effort to rest and allay her aunt's concern. She felt fine, but it appeared that those around her did not find her so. Especially when they thought she'd slept for more than ten hours.

After finishing with Muriel's outer garments, Aunt Penny began to remove her own. "There is your Aunt Mary and Constance—go at once and meet them. I shall be along shortly."

Muriel had the odd feeling she should make a special effort to appear cheerful this morning. The possibility that her secret might be close to discovery unnerved her. She needed to take more care.

"Good day, Aunt Mary, Constance," Muriel greeted her relatives.

"Good afternoon, dear Muriel." Aunt Mary's scrutinizing gaze was as keen as Aunt Penny's. "That is a beautiful day dress. Pomona green is a splendid color for you. It complements your hair and brings out your eyes."

"Yes." Muriel brightened her smile to demonstrate her enthusiasm, as false as it was. "It is one of my favorites. Aunt Penny and I chose this the first week we arrived in Town."

Constance, a picture in a rose-colored dress, linked her arm through her cousin's. "Let us continue, shall we? Her Grace wishes those of us who are to practice to meet with the dance master in the Saloon."

"It is quite probable that you will marry one of these young ladies," Lady Amhurst told Sherwin over her shoulder as she led the way to the Devonshire House Saloon. "You must make your greatest effort to be agreeable, Sherwin."

"Yes, Mother." Sherwin adjusted his sleeves, still distracted by the meaning of his encounter at the ruins. He could not bring himself to focus upon the present gathering.

Muriel hadn't seemed cross with him then. He remembered her cheeks flushed from the excitement of her discovery, the surprised expression, and her beauty . . . a long, soft curl brushing her smooth cheek. Her presence there proved she still held interest in what she'd once termed "all things Roman."

So who was this *Lady Muriel* who had come to London to find a husband? Surely not the same as the young woman who'd come to see the ruined Roman wall.

But she had arrived with that man at an unseemly early hour. Sherwin knew he should not trouble himself with Muriel's conduct, but the unusual circumstances were worrisome.

"Sherwin! Are you listening to me?" his mother scolded him, and rightfully so. He hadn't heard a word she'd said.

"Mama's right. That is a lovely frock." Constance glanced at Muriel's dress.

"Thank you, cous—" Muriel meant to return the compliment, but her cousin continued speaking.

"And you have every reason to want to look your best should you encounter him again. I suspect *he* will attend." They approached the open double doors of the Saloon. Constance leaned close to whisper, "The *on dit* is that there has been some sort of betrayal between the two of you—a love triangle, perhaps?"

"Do you mean to tell me the Earl of—" Muriel paused. Of course her cousin meant him. "What a load of rubbish. There is nothing of the sort."

"How else can you explain how it is that you two so often frequent the same places?" Constance's eyes went wide in accusation. "It is done out of spite, of course."

Their accidental meetings were no more than simply receiving, and accepting, the same invitations. She and the Earl had come across each other at a few parties, in the Park. Constance could not know, no one could know, about their meeting at the Roman wall that morning. Muriel still had some difficulty reconciling that her dear friend Sherwin Lloyd and Lord Amhurst were one and the same.

She missed him—Sherwin. Muriel had been trying her best to forget him, which proved difficult when she kept running into him. Then there were the times when she was alone, and thoughts of him came unbidden.

Her gaze drifted along the guests inside the Saloon. And there— Yes, she saw him. Muriel did her best not to look in his direction, and perhaps it was *too* noticeable that she never glanced to the east side of the room where he stood.

The soft murmurs eventually fell to hushed whispers. The Duchess of Devonshire bid a warm welcome to her guests and then introduced the dance master, Monsieur Gravois, who took charge at once.

Dark-haired, short, and slender, Monsieur Gravois sported a pointed moustache. His white shirtfront shone in stark relief to an otherwise all-black wardrobe. He stood with the bearing of a ballet dancer, extending his limbs and toes when he moved from one side of the room to the other. He chose ladies and gentlemen at random, indicating, with the end of his long baton, where they should stand in the square formation for the quadrille.

They first spent an inordinate amount of time correcting hand positions. The Monsieur walked up and down the

length of the room examining the various guests' appendages until he was satisfied.

Then they moved on to footwork. The guests endured
step-by-step critiques before the addition of slow music. Misplaced feet, heels, and toes were corrected. Soon the groups
moved in proper tempo across the floor. No one could say they
had not greatly improved.

All music, dancing, and instruction came to an end
when, several hours later, the Duchess of Devonshire inter-
vened.

"You've all done very well," the Duchess commented,
seemingly satisfied with the practice. "I doubt we shall repeat
the unfortunate incident at the Shropes' the other night. What
a disaster that was!" She put off all the bad feelings that the
faux pas invoked. "Let us move on to something new, shall
we?"

"Za valtz," the dance master announced.

"Waltz!" someone cried out.

"But, Your Grace," a timid yet brave Lady Emily ob-
jected. "I have not yet been given permission to dance that
at Almack's."

The Duchess turned her head in Lady Emily's direction,
presenting her with an imperious glare. "The Patronesses
of Almack's have no say here. Tonight you all shall be attending *my* party."

"I beg Your Grace's pardon." Lady Emily, who'd been
nudged repeatedly by her mother, sank into a deep curtsy.

"*C'est rien, enfant.*" A magnanimous smile spread over
the Duchess' lips. "We need a couple for demonstration pur-
poses." She gestured to the dance master. "*Monsieur!*"

Sherwin did not wish to be chosen. He had the irrational
thought that if he stood very still, perhaps he would not be

noticed. He stared at his hand, smoothing the sleeve of his jacket so as not to meet the gaze of either the dance master or the Duchess.

Monsieur Gravois spun to face the dancers. "*Mademoiselle?*" he called out to an unfortunate female he'd selected.

The Duchess took her time to stroll down the line of guests. Her Grace stopped when she reached . . .

"My lord?" She held out her hand to Sherwin.

He knew better than to refuse.

Sherwin accepted with a curt nod and took hold of the Duchess' proffered hand. His mouth had gone dry, and he could not speak. And how would he move forward to follow her? His legs felt heavy, and his knees refused to bend. He would be unable to walk behind the hostess, much less dance with the female Monsieur Gravois had chosen. And was he to dance alone before all these people? *He* was to be an example? This was embarrassment on a level he'd never imagined.

"Excellent. It is good to see our new earl is brave." The Duchess led him to the unoccupied portion of the room. There she turned him to face his partner.

Although he could not see her clearly, Sherwin had no doubt the lady before him was Muriel.

Chapter Seven

Her Grace the Duchess of Devonshire positioned the two of them together in the center of the floor. "Place your hand *there,* just like that—" She laid Sherwin's hand across Muriel's shoulder and hers over his. "Yes, that's right. Monsieur Gravois, come, *s'il vous plaît.*" She waved to the dance master to approach.

"Oui!" The delicate Frenchman appeared and joined the couple's free hands in front of them, Sherwin's above Muriel's. "We weel begin!" He instructed what each should do for the promenade. He then stepped closer to adjust their position, standing side by side where their arms arched over their heads. Monsieur barked, *"Les yeux!"*

Sherwin looked forward, meeting Muriel's gaze as ordered, and they gracefully stepped around each other in time to the baton thumping on the floor. They might have been alone in the large room, for no other sounds were heard. Not a whisper, a cough, or a sniffle from the guests.

"They're doing this on purpose," Muriel grumbled in clear dissatisfaction, staring straight ahead.

"For what reason?" Despite his embarrassment at being singled out and the only couple upon the dance floor, Sherwin was rather enjoying himself at the moment.

"We are on display for their amusement." Instead of becoming loud and animated, Muriel contained her ire, showing not a trace of what she felt. "All they want is to see us bicker."

"I find it difficult to believe you would allow anyone to make sport of you." After years of correspondence, Sherwin felt he had fair knowledge of her moods.

"*Droit,* monsieur, za right!" Monsieur Gravois corrected in a high, reedy tone.

Sherwin felt the dance master's baton tap his leg. Stepping to face Muriel, he brought his hand to rest at her waist.

"And you are certain I could contrive a plan to avoid humiliation?" Muriel placed her hands upon his shoulders.

"If anyone could, it would be you." Sherwin would be the first to admit he was not nearly as clever as she. No one was, actually. He quite admired her for it.

"And if my solution is one not to your liking, what then?" Muriel rotated around him, to his left.

"As well as you must know, I do not care for undue attention. I am amenable to any sensible solution." With an ear to the dance master's instructions, Sherwin's full attention centered on what Muriel would say next.

"Very well, if you give me a moment." She fell quiet and relaxed somewhat in his arms during her contemplation.

Sherwin slid his hand a fraction more toward her spine to secure his hold. He felt a bit self-conscious that he should touch her so intimately before all these people.

"We shall call a truce." She glanced up at him hopefully. "If we return to an amicable arrangement, there cannot be anything of interest for them to observe. We shall smile at each other and be pleasant."

"*Maintenant,* we begin again!" Monsieur Gravois announced with a quick double clap of his hands.

"An excellent idea. I knew a solution could be had once you put your mind to it." Sherwin pasted on his best effort, removed his left hand from her waist, and they returned to their original position to repeat the first steps again. "In any case, I have come to realize that I owe you an apology for that night we first met at Almack's."

He cleared his throat before taking her left hand in his and raising it above their heads for the pirouette. Although he stared into her face, he could not see her features clearly, only the green of her eyes.

Wasn't green the most beautiful color in existence? How had he ever thought otherwise?

"I believe we may have behaved in an unreasonable manner at our first encounter." Sherwin stepped around her as the Earth and moon rotated in the sky. "I was—am—just as guilty of omission as you. I had no right to accuse you of— In any case, I apologize for my rudeness and any embarrassment I might have caused. Perhaps I might have a chance to explain my behavior to you at a later date."

"I accept your apology and give you mine." Muriel admitted that it was silly for them to behave as if they were stubborn schoolchildren. They were not children anymore.

When she had first stood up with him, Muriel could not help but flinch at his touch. The longer they moved to the music, however, the easier it had become to accept the contact. He slid his arm around her waist and leaned close for her to place her hands upon his shoulders. Was it wrong that standing so close, touching him, did not now annoy her in the least?

Still, Muriel did not like how exposed she felt. Nervous

not because she was to dance before the other guests but because she had the distinct impression they would all know that she did not hate him. Not really, not anymore. She could not stay angry with him.

Although he had apologized for his actions, it seemed to Muriel that he did not care for her as he had previously, before their meeting at Almack's. They had enjoyed such an easy friendship. Their letters had always been of a pleasant nature over the years. If only they could return to that polite correspondence they'd once had—except all written communication had come to a halt. Muriel doubted she would ever receive another letter from him.

As much as he might have forgiven her, his opinion of her had clearly altered in recent days. That much was clear by his exceptionally polite attitude toward her. Any ease and geniality of their previous conversations, if only previously expressed in written form, were obviously not to return.

One ought to be grateful for the civility at least.

"I accept your apology," she repeated, "and I will gladly listen to your explanation." Muriel allowed her gaze to slide from her dance partner to the audience observing them. She considered how disappointed they would be not to see the couple before them at odds. What would they think if it were known that she actually took pleasure in dancing with him? It was a confession she did not wish to make to anyone. She did not even wish to admit it to herself. "Let us do what we can to defuse our current situation, shall we?"

Returning her attention to Sherwin, Muriel did her best to show the onlookers how delighted she was to dance with the Earl. She smiled at him as if he were the sun in their cosmic dance.

The guests appeared completely put out now that she and

Sherwin thoroughly enjoyed, or seemed to, each other's company. As shocking as it seemed, Muriel did. She could not, however, hazard a guess on her partner's behalf.

Soft grumbling and general discontented sounds came from the audience.

Muriel's smile widened in earnest. There was nothing she liked better than being right.

Almost an hour had passed, and Sherwin could not forget the adoring expression on Muriel's face. He only wished he could have seen it more clearly. What he could make out had caused warmth to spread outward from his chest, filling him with an overall blissful sense of well-being.

"I'm allowing you to visit the Egyptian Hall for an outing—pray, you do not ignore Miss Holbrook for some ancient stone sculpture." Lady Amhurst's voice broke through Sherwin's obscured vision. "I know how fond you are of antiquities."

He guessed the only way an ancient stone sculpture would be of any interest to Miss Holbrook was if it wore a fetching bonnet of superior quality, which was something he couldn't quite imagine.

"There!" Lewis announced.

"Very handsome," Lady Amhurst concurred. "Especially with that maroon paisley waistcoat."

Sherwin thought the selection a bit too funereal but said nothing. Lifting the quizzing glass hanging from the corded ribbon around his neck, he wished to reassure himself it was not forgotten. He was positive there would be something at the Egyptian Hall worth a closer inspection.

Sherwin had been correct. Standing across the street from the entrance of the Egyptian Hall some two hours later, he clearly saw that although Isis and Osiris wore Egyptian crowns, neither sported what Miss Holbrook would consider a fashionable bonnet.

"Are those the types of things you expect to see inside?" Miss Holbrook held on to Sherwin's arm and stared at the decorative doorway.

"I do believe you are correct, my dear." Sherwin felt unusually elated. "It is the *Egyptian* Hall after all."

The very opportunity to visit might have explained his added delight, but it was much more than that. Sherwin glanced around, expecting to see . . . what? He thought, he hoped, actually, he anticipated her presence—Muriel's.

From his position across the street, Sherwin spotted Muriel and Miss Susan Wilbanks, accompanied by the same two gentlemen they'd been out with on a drive a few days earlier. The foursome stood before the entrance, staring at the facade looming above them.

Muriel had the most uncanny ability to appear in the same place, at the same time, as he. He easily recalled her expression in the Park, at the Roman ruins, and at Hatchards Bookstore . . . .

He had watched her enter the bookstore, escorted by a young man whom Sherwin did not know. What he had noticed was Muriel's flush of excitement upon sight of the tall, endless bookshelves. She had not shown it outwardly, but he could see her eyes sparkle with interest. The young lady he'd brought, Lady Sophie, was clearly bored to tears when faced with the prospect of visiting the bookstore and fussed with her lace-ruffled sleeve.

Sherwin could not help noticing Muriel's indecision at whether or not to purchase a copy of a book she'd discovered. The manner in which she'd wrapped it in her arms told him of her precious find. In the end, for a reason not clear to him, she'd returned the book to its place on the shelf.

After she'd left, and when he was certain he would not be seen, Sherwin immediately retrieved the book to see the title, *Cursus Publicus: Roads of the Roman Empire,* and summarily purchased it. He treasured not only the information lying inside but now understood the real value the book held . . . *she* had touched the very same binding.

"Are you quite certain *this* is where you wish to visit?" Miss Holbrook's reservations were palpable.

Sherwin glanced at the lady on his arm. Perhaps it was best they not enter. To be seen so close to Muriel so soon after the Devonshire party that afternoon might cause more unwanted talk.

"Am I correct in assuming the Egyptian Hall does not hold any interest for you?" Sherwin offered her a smile and patted her gloved hand. "That's all right. I'm quite sure an ice at Gunther's is more to your taste."

This would be exactly the type of place she might find him frequenting. Muriel gazed around at the gathering crowd standing before the Egyptian Hall after she had looked her fill at the statues, ankhs, and various other creatures adorning the great entrance. He seemed to have the ability to turn up at the same place as she at the exact same time as she. If it were not for her notion that Sherwin might be near, Muriel might have enjoyed attending the museum for its own merits.

"Fascinating! This is simply astounding, do you not think, Lady Muriel?" Mr. Ambrose stared up at the towering Osiris and Isis and sounded quite sincere.

"Yes, indeed, sir, this is certainly an unequaled sight to behold," Muriel replied. She'd gazed the length of both sides of the street and did not see a sign of the Earl.

"You may find some of their lectures of interest, Lady Muriel. If you should think you would like to attend, pray, allow me to accompany you."

"Thank you. It is most kind of you to offer." Muriel might like to attend, but she felt certain her father would frown upon the very idea. Not that he had any objections to Mr. Ambrose, but he might fear that his youngest would slip back into her bookish ways. Muriel had not abandoned them; they were merely hidden. "I shall give the thought some consideration. Shall we proceed inside, sir?"

"Of course. I did not wish to continue before you ladies were ready." He looked to Susan and Mr. Stanley, who were discussing the massive ornate facade before them.

"I am sure I can speak for Miss Wilbanks that we are more than ready to move forward." Muriel had no doubt that what lay inside would prove interesting to her. Susan, on the other hand, might find the outing only tolerable.

If Muriel were to guess, what her friend truly enjoyed was being in the company of Mr. Stanley, no matter what their destination.

After returning Miss Holbrook to her residence, Sherwin sat in the barouche reminiscing over the time he had spent with Muriel that morning at Devonshire House. It had been very uncomfortable at first. But when he stood close to her, took her hand into his, touched her . . . A smile spread across his face. He could not deny it had been very pleasant.

Then he recalled that very afternoon at the Egyptian Hall. Muriel's astonished expression was not one he'd soon forget. Mr. Ambrose had not seemed nearly as impressed with the towering, marble-columned Isis and Osiris entrance as she. And whatever did she see in that man?

A bright glint woke Sherwin from his trance. The reflection of light from a fob, dangling from a gentleman's ribbon, caught his attention. Up ahead, walking along the street he traveled upon, were Mr. Ambrose and Mr. Stanley.

"Stop the carriage!" Sherwin had a burning desire to know where the two men were headed. He kneeled on the opposite bench and grabbed the driver's coat to gain his attention.

"I cannot, milord," the driver replied. "I has my orders from your lady mother." But the horses slowed. "I am to return directly to Lloyd Place at the conclusion of your afternoon drive."

The barouche had slowed enough for Sherwin to leap from the transport to the ground without injury. He called up to the driver, "Very well, then, you follow your orders. I would not wish to see you sacked on my account." He glanced at the two men across the street, making sure they remained in sight. Sherwin brushed off his trousers, straightened his waistcoat, and set the sleeves of his jacket to rights.

Then the carriage came to a full stop. Horse hooves and their jangling riggings nearly muffled the driver's reply. "What shall I tell her ladyship? She cannot like this, milord. I beg of you . . ."

"That will be my problem, won't it?" Sherwin would face that difficulty when it arrived, for his mother would not be pleased by his absence.

Mr. Ambrose and Mr. Stanley turned into a doorway and entered an establishment, which caused Sherwin to take immediate notice and end his discourse with the driver.

"How will you manage to find your way back to Lloyd Place?" the coachman called down to him.

"I cannot think about that now. All I know is that I will

manage." Sherwin had to move forward or lose the two gentlemen altogether. "I'll not have you disobey Lady Amhurst. Off with you!"

Sherwin crossed the barouche's wake after it moved down the street without him. He glanced at the building's white exterior and bow window before stepping inside.

"Lord Amhurst!" one of the staff members nearly shouted. With a shuffle of papers, a few others dashed around him, and a second steward called out, "Welcome to White's Gentlemen's Club!"

The dues had been paid, he was told, for a lifelong membership for the earls of Amhurst. Sherwin wasn't quite sure what he had stumbled into. White's Gentlemen's Club? All he knew was that Mr. Ambrose and Mr. Stanley had entered.

He strode down the carpeted hall and through a doorway, turned, and turned again through another portal, full of purpose but without knowledge of the destination.

What did Ambrose have that Sherwin lacked? Was he taller, more handsome, or better educated? Why would Muriel prefer the company of this man to Sherwin's?

Dash it! Sherwin glanced about. He was lost . . . yet again. He was only moments behind Ambrose and yet had managed to lose his quarry.

He stepped into a room where two young gentlemen stood at a hearth with drinks and cheroots, resting their feet on the fender. They straightened at Sherwin's sudden appearance and abruptly left.

No sooner had the young men departed than a trio of elderly gentlemen poked their heads out from around three tall leather chairs before getting to their feet and quitting the room.

No one wanted to be near him and the blue-devilled way he was feeling at the moment. The sentiment was reciprocal.

He clasped his hands behind his back and paced before the now-deserted, smoldering fireplace.

"I say . . ." A *sotto* voice interrupted Sherwin's solitude.

Sherwin turned, not to glare at the disturbance but to see who'd been brave enough to enter.

"Lloyd? Is that you?" A wavy-haired fellow strode into the room, fairly skipping.

Sherwin pivoted toward him for a better look. If the fellow got any closer, he'd appear as only a giant blur.

"Freddie?" He almost did not recognize the Earl of Brent outside of the walls of Eton. Two years Sherwin's senior, Muriel's brother, Freddie, had recently been graduated and had been acquainted with him for these last four years.

"It is you! What the devil—" Freddie glanced around the empty room. "You look a veritable thundercloud . . . and, by the by, what are you doing in Town?" He strode to his schoolmate and shook his hand. "Thought you had no stomach for the social scene, Lloyd."

"I don't, and it's Amhurst now, I'm afraid." He hated the sound of it and secretly dreaded it when people called him by that name.

"You're the new earl?" Freddie returned.

Sherwin answered with a curt nod. "Lost my brother Charles in the war last year, and both James and Father were carried off by influenza this past winter."

Freddie gave a sharp, low whistle. "Rum luck, ol' man." He clapped Sherwin on the shoulder.

A lump came to Sherwin's throat, and his eyes began to water. Freddie's clap had been the only physical contact he'd received to console him.

"Now you're saddled with the family responsibility. What wise words does Moo have for you?"

"I never told her of my circumstance." Sherwin tried to sound brave.

"Never?" Freddie turned to a sideboard to fill two glasses and held one out for Sherwin.

"No." Sherwin declined the spirits with a shake of his head.

"Does she know you're here in Town looking for a bride?" The question evidently was not an inquiry regarding Sherwin's purpose but whether or not Muriel knew of it.

Sherwin was taken aback. He hadn't mentioned anything about marriage.

"You'd surely be in deep mourning if the need for a wife was not imperative, my man." Freddie chuckled, then sipped from his glass.

"Just so," Sherwin acknowledged. "I made the mistake of not relaying those details to Moo—Lady Muriel. In my defense, she never mentioned her intention of coming to Town either. We met inadvertently at Almack's the other night, and, I must admit, we each surprised the other. There was a rather unpleasant row."

"In the middle of Almack's?" Freddie's eyes widened in surprise. "Well, Moo values honesty if nothing else. So I can see why she'd be upset."

"We're no longer at daggers drawn. Managed to patch things up for the time being. Hope it holds." Sherwin had no idea how things would be between them when next they met. Couldn't be any worse than it had been, really. "Have you seen her?"

"No, I haven't stopped at Worth House yet. Just got into Town and thought I'd wash a bit of traveling dust off before dropping in on the family." Freddie set his empty glass upon the table. "I knew you two exchanged letters. I thought you fancied her."

Perhaps Sherwin did, a little.

"No, there's nothing between us—not romantic—no, it's nothing like that." Sherwin felt his face grow warm. He knew there should not be any objection to the topics they discussed. Men had been called out and shot for the unsavory behavior of which Freddie spoke. And, being her brother, he'd be the one taking the initiative to restore his sister's honor.

"I believe you are in need of a friend," Freddie announced.

"I—I am in need of a *what*?" Sherwin stared at Freddie as best he could, although the Earl of Brent appeared as a hazy blob of brown.

"You need a male companion. Someone to set an example, show you how to be handy with your fives, punt on tick, watch that you don't stray into dun territory, and see to it that—"

"—I dress well?" Sherwin straightened with interest.

"Is there a problem with your wardrobe?" Freddie eyed Sherwin with less formality than Miss Torrington had last night. "Your clothing appears to be finely constructed."

"I didn't choose these. My mother did." It was a confession Sherwin hated to voice.

"Oh, I see your point." Freddie reached for the decanter and filled his glass.

"I think a man has a right to have a say about his own clothing, don't you?" Sherwin hadn't thought along these lines before Miss Torrington had raised the subject, but she had made a good point. "Not that I took any interest in my wardrobe before. My mother has taken care of such things for me."

"Haven't got a mother, but I should think a man's got to

learn how to fend for himself." Freddie sipped from his glass. "If taking a hand in choosing one's waistcoat isn't one of them, I'll be dashed."

"You will help me, then?" Sherwin had had no idea how much he needed the guidance of an older male. It was fortunate Freddie had come along.

"It's a male's prerogative, I should think." Freddie appeared set on the idea. "Don't have any brothers of my own, and you've lost yours recently. I'd be glad to lend a hand."

"I can't thank you enough, Freddie." Sherwin's chin lowered nearly to his chest. Even if his brothers were still alive, he wasn't sure he'd be experiencing such an outing with either of them.

"One thing, though." Freddie drained his glass and set it on the table. "You can't go on calling me *Freddie*. It's *Brent* from now on—best you remember that. We're not school-boys anymore, *Amhurst*."

Right enough. Sherwin motioned to the door. "Let's be off then, Brent."

Chapter Eight

Goodness—it's Freddie!" Aunt Penny's voice carried from the marbled foyer of Worth House down the corridors and probably to the attics.

Tall, dark, and handsome, Frederick, Earl of Brent, had his father's wavy hair but the dark coloring of his mother, a trait shared with his sisters Augusta and Muriel.

"Freddie!" Muriel called out, and she ran down the corridor to her brother.

"Aunt Penny, Moo." He greeted each with an embrace and a kiss on their cheeks.

The Duke soon joined them and held his hand out to his son. "Good to see you, Frederick."

Freddie grasped his father's hand, and they shook—like two real men. Even though Muriel had grown since she'd last seen him, Freddie stood much taller, and he looked, somehow, much older. Perhaps it was the stubble of whiskers on his wide jaw or the set of his broad shoulders that made a difference. It certainly was wonderful to see him again.

"Please tell me you're staying here with us," Muriel implored.

"Of course I'll stay, unless there are any objections," he teased. "Then I can set up at Clarendon's."

"This isn't quite a family reunion, but with Gusta in Suffolk and Char-Char in Cornwall, it will have to do."

"May I offer you a drink?" The Duke gestured that his son follow him.

Muriel fairly dragged her brother behind their father toward the library.

"I barely recognized you, Moo," Freddie teased her. "Look at you, in an honest-to-goodness frock with lace and ruffles, your hair in curls—I can hardly believe it! You might even attract a man, done up like that." He laughed and grew serious when he took a closer look. "You're more than passable—I suppose, you're not an antidote—quite pretty, actually."

"You're such a man of the world," she groaned. "And it's *Lady* Muriel now, my lord."

"*My lord,* is it?" Freddie lifted her and spun her around and around, making her squeal in a most unladylike fashion and making her terribly dizzy besides. "You're mighty haughty— dangerous with a bit of Town bronze."

His Grace poured into two glasses. "Moo, here, has even attended Almack's."

"You don't say!" Freddie gawked at her. "Why, you really have changed. No longer trying to alter hundreds of years of tradition at Eton? Have you left poor Headmaster Keate alone finally?"

Freddie knew very well that, without a formal education, she could not be admitted to a higher-education institution, whether or not it admitted females. Still, she would keep her matrimonial ruse even from her brother.

"Will you do me the favor of informing me which you plan to lay siege to, Cambridge or Oxford? And I'll make plans to attend the other."

Both Freddie and their father had a good laugh.

Muriel did not find that humorous in the least and made no effort to even pretend she was amused.

"Would you care for some Madeira?" The Duke offered his son a glass, which Freddie accepted. "Speaking of university . . . what are your plans for university?"

Freddie took a deep drink and glanced at Muriel, masking another teasing smile. "I thought I might take a year off and make a Grand Tour before making that decision."

Grand Tour! She willed herself not to react. Because any volatile outburst to her brother's announcement would surely give her away as the determined bluestocking she was.

The Continent. Europe. Italy. Muriel could not believe it. Freddie was going to Rome.

"How nice for you," she commented, sounding most pleased at his good fortune. "You lucky, lucky, boy." Muriel squeezed his arm in a playful manner . . . or perhaps not so playful. Then she pinched his cheeks.

"Watch it, there!" he cried out. "That hurts."

"Sorry." But she wasn't, really. "It's just that you're so *very* fortunate."

"Many in my position do the same." It was true that many young men traveled to Europe for firsthand exposure to foreign culture, architecture, and the arts.

"Yes, I know." Life was so unfair for girls.

"When do you plan to leave?" The Duke eased into the chair behind his desk.

"I thought I might remain in Town for Moo's Season," her brother replied. "Somehow I managed to miss Gusta's and Char-Char's altogether."

"They were completely uneventful," Muriel commented in a cool manner. "Both of them."

"My sisters are grown, and time is slipping by quickly." Freddie had missed much since he'd been away at school.

"I thought that was apparent only to me." Their father, who wasn't all that old, sounded as if he were fast approaching his dotage.

Muriel's failed Season would not be a disappointment to her or to His Grace.

"I'd be delighted if you'd save me a waltz next time you're at Almack's." Freddie's request sounded heartfelt.

"Of course." Muriel smiled and dipped into a shallow curtsy. "I'd be delighted."

"I cannot believe how much you have changed. Now you are a real lady. It's funny, really." Freddie chuckled. "I remember a time when you couldn't stand the thought of dancing."

The footman heralded, "The Earl of Brent," at the ballroom doorway of Devonshire House that evening.

The announcement came as a shock to Muriel. She hadn't thought her brother had received an invitation to the Devonshires' ball—but here he was.

Freddie stepped through the double-door portal and glanced about the room. Once he spotted Muriel, there was no stopping his progress to share her company.

"What are you doing here?" She regarded her brother's slightly rumpled attire. He was wearing the very same clothes he'd worn that afternoon! "I'm quite certain you bespoke a dance at Almack's. I had no idea you were to attend tonight's ball."

Muriel had been busy looking for Lord Caldwell, who was to partner her for the next set. Across the room she spot-

ted Sherwin, making what she thought was a fairly incon-
spicuous attempt to capture her attention. Was it wrong of
her to wish to communicate with him rather than stand up
with Lord Caldwell or converse with her brother, who stood
waiting at her side? She could not say exactly what had
changed her opinion of him or when it had happened. But
to Muriel, Sherwin now seemed the best choice of companion by far.

He moved his mouth, forming words that she deciphered:
Do you think we should share a dance this evening?

"I hadn't meant to, but I've heard—" Freddie turned to
see what had captured Muriel's attention.

Muriel's answer to Sherwin was just as silent. *After what
the Duchess put us through this morning, I think it would
be a good idea. I would hate to disappoint everyone.* She
snickered, unable to believe she actually looked forward to
dancing. It was so unlike her.

Freddie acknowledged Sherwin with a slow nod. "Good
Gad, don't tell me Amhurst participates in that speech-
reading nonsense as well."

"It's far more private than sending a footman around
with a *billet doux*." Muriel felt quite certain her brother re-
sented the ability because it was one he could not master.

"From what I hear, you'd know all about that." Freddie was
behaving very peculiarly. It was as if he was privy to some
secret.

She sincerely hoped it was not hers.

"I've just come from—" He began very anxiously but
came to an abrupt halt.

What was that smell? Muriel sniffed, trying to discern
the scent. Cigar smoke? Spirits?

"Never mind where I've been." Freddie seemed to choose
his words carefully to avoid any accusations. "The point is

that I heard from—" He stopped again. "It doesn't matter who told me—"

"Oh, do get on with it," she urged him, growing more impatient as time went on. "Lord Caldwell will arrive to claim his dance soon."

"He may not wish to keep your company once he learns that you are meeting a man without the benefit of a chaperone." Freddie sounded cross and yet, at the same time, unexpectedly protective. "I take it he is no gentleman if you must steal off to see him."

It shocked Muriel that he knew. How did he . . . How?

"Suffice it to say, I *do* know of your sordid activity, and if it were to come to Father's attention . . . I cannot even imagine what he should do to either of you."

"I have no idea what you have heard or from whom. I will say that you, and your source, could not be more incorrect." She would deny the accusation to her father as well. Muriel had done nothing of which she should be ashamed. It was all a lie. "There is no 'sordid' anything."

"Mind your tongue, Moo."

"I suggest you take stock of your own behavior before you go pointing fingers at others, Freddie." She glared at him from toe to head, leaning closer to him to whisper, "Appearing at Devonshire House, disheveled, smelling of cheroot smoke and drink, and, to top it off, uninvited, would cause more of a scandal than I ever could produce." Then, spotting Lord Caldwell off to the right, she walked away to greet him.

Sherwin quite considered he had done his duty by standing up with Miss Holbrook and Miss Torrington. He sought out Muriel for their waltz.

"Good evening, Lady Muriel." He bowed and reached

for her proffered gloved hand. "I cannot tell you how much I have looked forward to this moment."

"Doing it too brown, are we not, Lord Amhurst?" Muriel reprimanded him. "We should keep our behavior cordial if we wish to appear believable."

"What makes you think I am not sincere?" He felt an unexpected shiver at the touch of her hand. Suddenly, for the first time in any female's company, he felt as awkward and nervous as he had at thirteen.

The expression of disbelief she bestowed upon him was one he had not seen in a very long time. At that moment he recognized a bit of the Muriel he'd remembered: a perceptive, keen, and clever girl.

"Where's your brother?" Sherwin would have known Freddie even at this distance. He'd be the only gentleman in attendance who sported top boots and a frock coat at a ball. "I did not know he was to attend tonight."

They had spent the majority of the afternoon together visiting boot makers, haberdashers, and several tailors. Freddie had lent counsel on Sherwin's purchases for his wardrobe. Sherwin had found the whole experience eye-opening.

Who knew there was a skill to dressing like an earl?

"He dropped by with the express purpose of aggravating me," Muriel replied. "I believe a brother's sole goal in life is to vex his sisters. This one's is, in any case."

"That cannot be true. I shan't believe it. Freddie is the very best of fellows." Sherwin led Muriel to the dance floor and stood in almost the exact place they had that morning. "Do you think it odd that we are dancing the waltz?" This was, after all, their first public, and the most intimate, dance. Somehow, to him, it seemed as if it should be considered scandalous behavior.

"We spent nearly an hour practicing this morning." Muriel placed her left hand on his shoulder and extended her right hand, waiting for him to take hold. "It would be disappointing if we did not participate, much less lead the dance."

"I suppose." Sherwin placed his left hand over her right, taking her fingers into his. As he waited, he became aware of the position of his right hand upon her shoulder, dangerously close to the nape of her neck. He would have felt the soft, curling tendrils of her auburn hair brushing the back of his hand if he wasn't wearing gloves.

"Sherwin!" Muriel whispered with some urgency. She wiggled the fingers of both hands, attempting to gain his attention. "The music begins!"

"I beg your pardon." He moved forward in the steps of the *marche*.

What was wrong with him? The very idea that he would have had such a thought about her shocked him. He never had a notion regarding femininity about any young lady. So why, he wondered, had this happened with Lady Muriel?

The Earl of Brent's arrival the next morning at Lloyd Place came as something of a surprise to Sherwin. He had told Sherwin they needed to return to the tailor for a final fitting, especially if any of the waistcoats were to be completed by the morrow. Sherwin wasn't quite sure how Freddie had accomplished the deed, but he had convinced Mr. Weston to complete no less than three for the next day.

After being introduced, Freddie strode to the coffee urn on the sideboard in the breakfast room.

"Morning, Amhurst. Mind if I help myself?" He filled a cup and pulled up the chair next to Sherwin. "You look more like yourself when you're wearing those."

Sherwin adjusted his spectacles and closed the book he'd been reading.

"We're off to Weston's after you've finished, right?" Freddie snagged a piece of toast from the rack sitting in the center of the table and bit the corner.

"Ah . . . I haven't informed my m—" The struggle, Sherwin anticipated, would be in convincing Lady Amhurst to allow him to accompany Freddie and not her for morning calls.

"Look here, ol' man," Freddie lectured around the bite of toast. "You are the Earl. She's, at best, the Dowager Countess. I don't know what's going to happen once you marry, but if you don't want your new Countess to rule the roost, you'd best start crowing yourself now."

Sherwin lowered the forkful of breakfast from his mouth. The poultry metaphors caused him to feel a bit guilty about consuming his buttered eggs. "I'm not sure I entirely understand your meaning, Brent."

Lady Amhurst appeared at the doorway. Freddie scrambled to his feet with military precision. Sherwin followed seconds later. He'd never risen when his own mother entered the room before.

"Good morning, your lordship." She sank into a shallow curtsy. "Welcome to Lloyd Place."

"Lady Amhurst, I am delighted," Freddie replied. "Will you join us?"

"No, thank you. I am curious, though. Might I inquire as to the reason for your call?"

"Amhurst and I are running a few errands this morning. Not a problem, I trust." Freddie stared at her in a calm fashion with raised eyebrows. Had he been expecting some objection? An argument? A resounding refusal?

"We had planned to pay some calls, but I expect we can dispense with that formality today." Lady Amhurst's voice became a steely monotone.

Sherwin could tell his mother wasn't happy about the alteration in the day's plans. Especially since she wasn't the one making the changes. What would she do if *he* took such a position with her? On occasion she would lose her temper. If he opposed her, would she lash out at him with more than angry words? Dare she strike him? Worse?

"Thank you for your kind indulgence. I bid you good day, then." Freddie—no, the Earl of Brent—had excused Lady Amhurst!

Sherwin had never seen his mother submit to anyone other than his father, who had been . . . the previous earl. Yet he saw anger and resentment underneath her quiet facade. How her displeasure would exhibit itself, he could not imagine.

Freddie waited until she left to return to his seat. "You've got to understand, Sherwin, that you hold the rank of an earl. There is an entitlement and respect due to both parties, you for her, and she for your new position. Lady Amhurst might find it difficult to adapt, but she must realize that you are no longer merely her son."

It was something he must have known, but Sherwin had never really thought on it much.

"If you don't stand up to your mother now, you can't very well expect your new wife to do so, can you? Unless you married someone like Muriel. She'd see fit to put your house in order, all right." He chuckled and sipped his coffee.

Sherwin finally managed to eat his buttered eggs from his fork.

Freddie then fell silent and said thoughtfully, "The two of you have always rubbed along well. Why don't you marry her?"

"Marry Moo?" Sherwin nearly choked. His eyes watered and went wide. "Are you mad?"

"It was just a suggestion." Freddie shrugged. "I expect you could do a lot worse."

Sherwin stared back, when it occurred to him that Freddie was not mad in the least.

He was brilliant. A blooming genius!

Chapter Nine

That afternoon Sherwin drove through Hyde Park with Miss Shrope. Whether the day was exceptionally fine or not, he had no idea, for Freddie's notion that he should marry Muriel had not been forgotten. The idea was one Sherwin could not easily rid himself of, and, as the hours passed, he spent more and more time considering its merits. Sadly, he had to admit he was not very attentive to his companion.

"Do you search for Lady Muriel? Is it she you favor?" Miss Shrope sounded somewhat distant, as though she knew rather than simply suspected.

Sherwin looked at her but said nothing. Apparently his expression told her whatever she needed to know.

"That really is most unfortunate. Oh, no!" Her small gloved hand covered her lips moments after her *faux pas*. "I beg your pardon, my lord. I had not meant to say that."

"Why do you say 'unfortunate'?" Sherwin dreaded what might come next.

"It is only that— Oh, I dislike gossip." She made a most

disagreeable expression, which reinforced his concern that what Miss Shrope knew, what she was about to tell him, might be alarmingly unpleasant. "You know they call you the catch of the Season, do you not? Any young lady would be flattered if you were to show her interest."

Yes, he understood that every matchmaking mama wanted to snare him for her daughter, and every eligible miss seemed to cast lures in his direction. He might have been easily snared if his own mother, aided by the ever-observant Mr. Gibbons, hadn't been watching with such keen interest, making sure Sherwin sidestepped the traps.

"If only you would turn your attention to someone else, someone more worthy." It sounded more like a plea than a suggestion.

"Why? What is it you're not telling me?" Sherwin truly did not wish to hear further gossip concerning Muriel. On the other hand, he must learn what it was people were saying about her.

She glanced away from him. "I do not wish to upset you, my lord."

"Please, I wish you to tell me." He all but begged her.

"What they are saying may not be true." She still resisted and would not look directly at him.

"I still wish to know, if you please." Sherwin did not know any more he could say to convince her. He waited patiently, hoping she would accede.

"Very well. If you insist. I—" Miss Shrope drew in a slow, deep breath before she began. "Last night I heard that Lady Muriel meets with someone."

"'Someone'?" Sherwin whispered to himself, finding it difficult to believe such a thing.

"Without her aunt or her father's knowledge." Miss Shrope

began to cry. Relaying the rumor, knowing it injured Sherwin to hear the words, obviously pained her as well. "No one knows who he is or where they meet."

"How do you know this to be true, then?" Sherwin uttered the words, but he did not recognize his own strained voice.

"I do not—not for certain, that is. That is why I detest gossip. It could be completely untrue. See how it wounds you." Miss Shrope blinked up through her tear-moistened lashes. "If only you would favor a more suitable young lady, there are many who would look upon you with . . ."

The image of the young man following Muriel into the Roman ruins from days ago came to mind. Apparently Sherwin had not been the only one who'd seen them, and the thought of her keeping company with an undesirable fellow . . .

"Never fear, Miss Shrope." Sherwin patted her hand, trying to lend her some comfort. "I cannot will my affection from one to another, but I shall not give my favor to anyone unworthy. Rest assured, I shall obtain a satisfactory resolution."

With satchel in hand, Muriel strode into the marbled foyer of Worth House and informed Susan of her change of plans. It seemed as of late that Muriel had difficulty rising early to study. She had trouble rising because she had difficulty falling asleep at night. Her mind was preoccupied with thoughts of Sherwin. The new Earl of Amhurst had become a constant and unexpected distraction to her.

She hadn't increased the number of lessons as she had hoped. Muriel did what she could and managed to make some last-minute arrangements.

"I am to meet with Signore Biondi this afternoon."

"You don't mean now?" Susan cried, sounding heartbroken. She held the newly crafted bonnet she'd been working on for a good portion of the week. "But Sir Samuel is to take us for a drive."

"Sir Samuel will still take us for a drive, goose." Muriel continued in a whisper. "Only there will be an additional stop."

"Does he know?"

"We'll tell him as soon as he arrives." Muriel retrieved her favorite poke bonnet, smoothed her hair, and placed it upon her head. Their outing would not be altered. The coach would simply make an unscheduled stop, dropping Muriel off, and continue on with Susan and Sir Samuel. No harm would be done, and no one would be the wiser.

"If you wear that, you will be instantly recognized." Susan held out her new Capucine-colored silk, wide-brimmed hat with a delicately arching ivory-colored ostrich plume. "You should wear mine. No one has seen it yet."

Susan pulled Muriel's bonnet from her hands and exchanged it with her own. Before the echoes of the knock at the front door faded, Susan, who had just slipped on her Spencer, was there to greet Sir Samuel.

"Are you ladies ready?" The Baronet stepped inside and waited patiently.

"Certainly." Susan had finished tying the ribands under her chin and accepted Sir Samuel's proffered arm. Walking out the front door, she glanced over her shoulder at her friend.

"You go ahead," Muriel urged them. "I'll be ready by the time you return, Sir Samuel."

"Don't be all day about it," he replied, and he escorted Susan to his waiting carriage.

Muriel found Susan's hat difficult to don. She thought the weight of the bonnet unwieldy and would vow she could feel the feather soaring above her head. And how, Muriel wondered, would no one notice her when she wore this?

Sherwin returned Miss Shrope much sooner than either had expected. They did not see much point in continuing their outing or their conversation. She'd fallen into a melancholy he could not alleviate.

He started back on the journey home. While staring off to one side, he saw, from a great distance, a gentleman escorting a lady to his carriage. From the movement, the way she swung her arms by her sides, and the gait, the lady, he was certain, was Muriel.

"Stop! No—turn around! There!" he called out to the coachman, pointing to the opposite side of the square.

"You're wantin' to stop off at 'anover Square, sir?" The jangling of the horses' harness grew to an almost unbearable din when the coachman reined them in.

"Yes, around the outside of the circular path," Sherwin instructed. "Pull up on the far end, and keep quiet."

At this distance Sherwin could clearly see it was Muriel in an astonishingly fancy bonnet. With his bonnet knowledge, bestowed upon him by Miss Holbrook, he knew that the effort it took to fashion such a creation would be immense. This man accompanying Muriel must surely be one she cared for greatly, unlike Mr. Ambrose or Lord Peter.

Sherwin also felt this was the very same gentleman he had seen earlier at the Roman wall. Who was he?

Muriel stepped up into the carriage, the man followed, and the door closed. Soon the black carriage moved off. The long feather atop her head poked out the window and seemed to be waving at Sherwin, beckoning him to follow.

So be it.

"Follow them," he ordered the coachman.

"I beg your pardon, my lord, but my orders were—"

Sherwin followed his friend the Earl of Brent's example and leaned forward on the bench seat, exerted the privilege of his rank, and for the first time in his life barked out an order. "I said, follow that carriage."

The barouche shot forward, knocking Sherwin back into the seat. They headed out of Mayfair, down streets and city intersections he would never be able to identify. He had no idea where he was. After a good twenty minutes or so, the carriage they followed slowed, coming to a stop.

"Walk on," Sherwin instructed. "Turn the corner, and come about. Don't lose sight of them."

"Aye, my lord," the coachman answered without a hint of refusal. By the time the barouche came around and rolled to a stop, the black carriage had dropped off its occupants and continued on its way.

With foliage obscuring his view, Sherwin could only catch a glimpse of the long feather on Muriel's hat every now and again. She, and whoever else accompanied her, had descended from the carriage and crossed to a building. All traces of the plume disappeared once she stepped inside.

The deep, heavy weight Sherwin felt in his stomach worsened. He must follow her. He would find out exactly what was going on and whom she was meeting.

"*Uno minuto.*" Signore Biondi raised his hand and shook his index finger in Muriel's direction. "We shall begin the lesson after I return. *Scusi.*" He retreated into a hallway behind his carved desk. Muriel could see the back of his balding head and hear the swish from the hem of the long, heavy, dark maroon banyon.

Muriel settled onto her customary seat and emptied her satchel, setting her notepad, various papers, and books upon the small table next to her instructor's massive desk. She reached into the bag to locate her last item. Her fingers scuttled around the bottom for the short pencil.

The sound of someone entering the room through the open door from the narrow corridor behind her alarmed her. She straightened and spun in her chair to face the visitor.

"Muriel!"

"Sherwin?" She rose from her chair and could not have been more surprised to see him. "W-what are you doing here?"

"Where is he?" Sherwin demanded, glancing from one corner of the room to the other. His gaze finally settled on the darkened, narrow exit behind the desk. "I know he's here—the fellow who brought you."

"Brought me? The one who . . ." Muriel finally understood that he meant Sir Samuel. No, he wasn't there. He'd had no reason to remain. He and Susan would continue on their proposed drive without Muriel until it was time to collect her after the Latin lesson. "I'm afraid I will not reveal his identity."

"Then it's true." The realization washed across the Earl's face. "You've been deceiving your family into believing you care about making a match, and you've been toying with your suitors to tryst with *him*."

Was he still referring to Sir Samuel? What gave him the idea that . . .

"Well, my lord, what will you do?" Muriel would not be tricked into exposing Sir Samuel's involvement. "Expose my secret? Ruin my reputation? Disgrace my family? Create a scandal? The entire notion that I'm taking part in an illicit association is ridiculous."

"You do not deny that you are meeting with him?" Sherwin inched forward as he spoke. "You will not even say who he is." He sounded more than concerned; he sounded angry.

Muriel moved behind Signore Biondi's desk to put space between them. "I do not name him because I have no wish to punish his involvement in this venture when he is all that is kind by coming to my aid."

"All of London is talking about your indiscretion." Now Sherwin sounded outright jealous.

"My mistake," she uttered calmly. "I thought we agreed they were gossiping about *us* and what was going on between *us*."

Their mutual silence stretched on for a long while. They stood there, glaring at each other. Muriel did not understand the reason for his outburst. Why blame Sir Samuel when it was Sherwin who had introduced Signore Biondi to her?

Her pulse quickened, and the excitement mixed with anger, twisting inside her, making it difficult for her to think. "If you could only hear yourself. I would expect you to be the one person who'd understand." Tears came to Muriel's eyes, and she did not know why. She never cried. "Do you not realize? Look around you. Do you honestly not know where you are?"

He blinked, then squinted before lifting his quizzing glass to take a closer look at the completely filled bookcases, the extra tomes stacked on the floor against the walls. "This is . . ." Sherwin's angry expression faded when, as she suspected, he recognized his surroundings.

Signore Biondi appeared out of the small dark opening behind his desk. "Ah, another visitor. *Buon giorno!*"

"Signore Biondi, it is Sherwin Lloyd." Sherwin inclined his head. A flush rose into his face at the recognition of his error.

"He is now the Earl of Amhurst," Muriel added in a sharp tone, feeling acutely cross with him.

"*Si,* ah—*si!*" Signore Biondi nearly shouted and raised his hands high in welcome. "It has been many years since we have met, no? And I think there has been much that has happened between you two, yes?"

Muriel glanced over to Sherwin, who returned her slightly guilty glimpse. Their correspondence, albeit innocent, would never have been considered correct.

"I shall leave you two to your . . . discussion." Signore Biondi shrugged and readjusted his banyon around his shoulders. "*Amore,*" he mumbled to himself. "The English, what do they know?"

"I beg your pardon?" Muriel wasn't sure she had heard correctly.

"We Italians invented love!" He shook his finger at them before returning to the small corridor behind his desk. "Remember, children, *amor animi arbitrio sumitur, non ponitur.*" Then he left.

"What does he mean?" As if their situation wasn't difficult enough, Muriel saw no need for cryptic phrases to further confuse matters.

" 'We choose to love, we do not choose to cease loving,' " Sherwin translated.

"I understand *what* he said. But I cannot see how it has anything to do with us." Muriel had no wish to continue their "discussion." It was taking up her precious lesson time.

"So you've been secretly tutored." Sherwin must have finally understood what she had done.

"And you must know my father would not approve of my being here, nor would my aunt." Muriel began to relax and moved out from behind the desk. "I must deceive them for my education, if I am to see Signore Biondi at all."

"Yes, yes, of course . . ." Sherwin seemed relieved and at the same time disappointed in himself for the lapse.

"What does any of it matter?" Muriel was well aware of his daily presence in the Park, with a different young lady every day, and his highly anticipated, much-touted attendance at every evening affair. He probably did not give her a second thought. "I am nothing to you."

Their waltz last night could not have meant anything more to him than it had to her. The purpose was to quash annoying rumors. Muriel would never admit that she had, not in the smallest amount, enjoyed their dance, enjoyed the feeling of his arms around her, of him holding her close. She had enjoyed herself so very completely.

"Nothing? You could not be more wrong." Sherwin's voice softened, and he moved very slowly toward her. "I know there have been difficulties between us, especially that first time we met here in Town."

Muriel hated to think of that night at Almack's. Never had she felt more angry in her life. It wasn't too long after that, though, that her feelings had changed. She wasn't so vexed anymore. He was, after all, the very same Sherwin she had corresponded with for many years.

"You are . . . you mean, the world to me," Sherwin stated in a clear voice, without a hint of torment or mockery.

Muriel somehow knew he was telling her the truth. But she could hardly believe it. Was it possible he had forgiven her? Not only forgiven, but held her in great affection?

"I imagine we were both hurt; I know I was," he confessed. "We thought we'd been completely honest with each other—and I believe we had been, except for that which we'd omitted. It's only, we hadn't expected that our own actions, our each coming to London, would affect the other. How would we have known?"

Muriel had thought him at Eton, and it had never occurred to her he would visit London for the Season. So why
tell him of *her* visit? How lowering to confess that she would
pretend to stand in the petticoat line. Going to Town alleg-
edly to seek a husband? How could she possibly write to
him of that?

"Our years of correspondence were my happiest. Everything changed when my father and brothers died." He turned
away from her to sit on the edge of the desk. "All I cared
about was my studies and your letters. Now I'm the Earl. I
have to manage the estates, find a wife, marry and . . ." He
closed his eyes. "I hate my new life. My mother brought me
to Town and has me courting a countless number of young
ladies, none of whom I care for in the slightest." The mus-
cles of his jaw tightened, showing his irritation. "I could not
write to you of these things. I should have confided all to
you. I sincerely regret it now."

Muriel remained silent and listened to his tale. The longer he spoke, the more she empathized with him. Coming
to Town had at least been her choice; it had not been his.

"Only since I've seen you—" He opened his eyes and
faced her. "I have to confess that all I can think of is you.
Where you are and, even though it pains me, who it is sharing your company. It has taken me quite some time to realize how dear you are to me." Sherwin took her hand lightly
in his. "I cannot bear the thought of being apart from you.
If I must marry, I very much want it to be you."

"What?" Muriel could not have heard him correctly.

"We'll make the Grand Tour for our wedding trip." Excitement shone on his face, lighting up his eyes, animating
him. "Perhaps we'll travel straight to Italy. I daresay we've
both shared that interest for ages. We shall go to Rome and
stay for as long as you like. A year, no—two!"

Of course Muriel wished to see Rome. It was her fondest desire. But—

"If after Rome you wish to continue to Greece, we shall depart immediately. All you need do is say the word."

Muriel blinked and did not know what to make of this. He wished to *marry* her? This was all so very sudden.

"Is that a proposal?" She could hardly believe what she was hearing and could not help but tease him a bit. "It's not very romantic, is it?"

"As far as I know, you're not a very romantic sort of girl," he stated evenly.

"And you know me so well, don't you?" Muriel had to admit, she wasn't the highest stickler when it came to propriety. Actually, in most cases, she cast the whole idea aside . . . why had she thought it mattered now?

"Yes, I believe I do." Sherwin smiled first, and Muriel soon followed.

Still, what made him think she would ever accept such a casual, offhanded offer?

They weren't children anymore, and no one made Muriel realize it better than the grown Sherwin, the Earl of Amhurst.

"You're right, I'm not very romantic." She spied him out of the corner of her eye. He understood her very well.

"I adore you, Moo." Sherwin's smile widened, and he pressed her hand. "My search for a bride has ended. There is no one else for me. If you think on it, you'll know we belong together."

The declaration still shocked her. He sounded certain where his heart lay. It hadn't occurred to Muriel until that moment how deeply she had buried her feelings. She had been convinced he had absolutely no interest in her. But she did care for him.

"This is not why I came to London. I had no expectations of marriage," she confessed. "I did everything to discourage any of my suitors from reaching the point of offering."

"*I* was never one of your suitors. I have only a passing acquaintance with your family, and I have yet to pay even a courtesy call on you." For someone who did not appear interested in courtship, he seemed to know exactly what was proper and how to go about it. "We shall remedy that at once. I realize all this is new and sudden, but you shall come to realize, just as I did, it is meant to be."

"I cannot say no," she confessed.

He placed a kiss on the back of her gloveless hand. The feeling of his lips upon her skin caused Muriel's breath to catch. The pencil stub that she held in her left hand slipped from her fingertips, hit the carpet, and rolled across the floor.

"For now our engagement is secret—*sub secreto*," he told her. "But it shall not remain so for long."

Muriel stepped near and slid into his arms, where he held her close. This was so very right. This was where she belonged. How could she ever have thought that there could be anyone except Sherwin for her?

Chapter Ten

Sherwin's purpose for coming to Town had suddenly become perfectly clear. It had taken some time for the chaos that had come with the death of his father and brothers to ebb, but finally he felt at peace. Every element, every aspect of Sherwin's life had fallen into place, just as if it had been preordained.

"Is there cause for celebration?" Signore Biondi had reentered his study in silence. "I see the *signorina* has left. She appeared most felicitous, even though she has missed her lesson."

Gazing at Muriel was like looking into a mirror, Sherwin realized. She reflected every affection and good feeling inside of him. How he would remain sane until he could see her, be near her again, Sherwin did not know.

"I am quite overwhelmed," Sherwin replied. "I do not have the words, in any language, to express myself."

"Of course it is so. You are not fluent in Italian!" Signore Biondi shrugged. "Ah! I have something for you. *Attesa qui per uno momento.*" He drew his banyon to one side, out of the way, and settled in his chair, then pulled open one of his desk drawers and rummaged around. "I have always known, even when the two of you were both young. *Si, destino!*" Closing one drawer and opening another, the Signore continued his search. "Something very special, oh, yes, I knew even back then." He pulled the desk drawer open and proclaimed, "*Ecco!*"

Lying in the palm of Signore Biondi's hand was a small, round miniature painting set in a gold pendant. Sherwin lifted his quizzing glass to examine the image. It was a profile of Muriel—her eye, eyebrow, surrounded by wisps of her brown hair.

"Hand painted on ivory. I completed it many days ago, and just in time, I believe." Signore Biondi handed the gold-framed miniature to Sherwin. "It is a gift for you, *per favore.*"

"You painted this?" It was a perfect rendition. The auburn hue of her curls, the arch of her brow, the shape of her eye, and even the individual lashes. He'd even managed to catch her impish manner in the glint in her eye.

"I must occupy myself with something while the *signorina* works her lessons, so I sketch." He leaned over Sherwin's arm to regard his work. "I have some talent, do I not? It is good, yes?"

"It's an astonishing resemblance." He retrieved the empty fob from his waistcoat and fastened the portrait for safekeeping.

"You can keep her near even when you are apart." Signore Biondi nodded in a knowing manner. "Italians truly understand such things—and I think now that you do also, yes?"

"Thank you, Signore." Sherwin slipped the miniature into

his pocket, wishing the portrait lay even closer to his heart. "I shall treasure it always."

Muriel stepped down from the carriage, continued up the walk, passed through the front door of Worth House the moment it swung open, and came to a stop just short of running into the large round table in the marbled foyer.

She hadn't even paused once. It was just like magic.

"What is wrong with you, Moo?" Susan finally caught up and removed her hat, then untied Muriel's because she had not moved to do so. "You haven't said a word the entire drive home."

Muriel shrugged. How could she explain to Susan about the lighthearted, flighty sensations like butterflies filling her stomach, tickling her insides? Never before had Muriel felt so happy.

"And you have the most peculiar expression. Whatever are you about?"

Muriel wasn't thinking of anything in particular. Complete happiness and images of Sherwin filled her soul. Gazing at the bonnet Susan had lent her, Muriel mused that it wasn't as silly as she'd first thought, the color not so garish, the roped trim not as overdone but rather tastefully adorned, and the gently arching ostrich feather was rather artfully graceful.

All in all she found it rather quite splendid.

"Gracious, Moo!" Susan took her friend by the arm. "What ails you? Your eyes may be open, but I believe you are sleeping on your feet. If I tell your aunt as much, she would insist you proceed directly to bed and make sure you stayed there until morning."

"Oh, no—I must attend tonight!" If she missed the ball,

she would not see Sherwin, and Muriel did so wish to meet with him and, she hoped, dance with him. How she longed for him to hold her in his arms again.

"Moo, are you quite sure you're feeling all right?" Susan pulled the hat from Muriel's hand.

Muriel twirled away; maybe she spun twice. Oh, she did feel silly. Is this what it felt like to be in love? Life was wonderful, perfect.

"I'm fine, Sukey." Muriel relished her lovely secret and smiled. She was engaged to be married to the most wonderful man in all of Britain. "Actually, I've never been better."

Sherwin found preparation for the Burnettes' ball that evening bearable. He knew he would see his beloved, dance with her, and, most important, take the first step in securing her position as the new Countess of Amhurst.

He had tried to speak to his mother upon returning to Lloyd Place, but she had been unavailable. Sherwin would not allow much more time to pass. He would speak to her on their way to the ball tonight or at the ball, if need be.

While standing with his chin slightly elevated as Lewis did his magic, turning a strip of linen into a fashionable cravat, Sherwin thought back to the events of that morning: his meeting with Muriel, their heated discussion, which turned into a warm conversation, and finally to their secret engagement.

Sherwin truly hadn't been sure exactly how she would react to his declaration. What he had known was that he had to confess his affection for her. It seemed that once he'd started, he could not stop talking. He'd had to tell her how much he esteemed her, held her in regard, and completely treasured her.

He must have worn her down. She had said yes. Muriel had agreed to marry him.

He'd been walking on air when he finally left Signore Biondi's residence to return to Lloyd Place. As if by fate, Freddie had dropped in and was just about to leave. Sherwin was ever so glad to regale his proposal and its outcome.

"My word . . ." the Earl of Brent drawled in obvious surprise. He suggested Sherwin send a small but meaningful token of affection, an engagement gift, as it were.

It was a splendid idea, and Sherwin told him what he had in mind, and, by golly, if Freddie didn't know where the exact thing could be found.

The crafting of the neck cloth was a success on the first try. Lewis held up the waistcoat, slipped it over Sherwin's arms, settled it on his shoulders, and made the proper adjustments before fetching the jacket.

Sherwin's admiration had not been misplaced. He'd looked up to Freddie at Eton and continued to do so in London. It would be a great pleasure to call him brother after marrying Muriel.

Standing before his full-length mirror in his bedchamber, he regarded his refection. The gold-shot Burgundy-colored waistcoat was neither his first choice nor his second. Sherwin had wanted to sport one of the new garments he'd purchased, again with the guidance of Freddie. Unfortunately, none of them was ready for wear. He had wished to appear at his best for *her.*

Sherwin allowed Lewis and Lady Amhurst to make the decisions for this evening. The valet could labor over as many neck cloths as needed to achieve success, brush all the lint from every inch of his garments, and take an inordinate amount of time fussing with the accessories. Sherwin knew he would place the final and most important item on his person: the miniature portrait of Muriel.

Muriel stood next to Susan in the Burnettes' ballroom. She admired the simplicity of the Roman ruins depicted on the beveled window of her carved ivory *brisé* fan.

"That's new, isn't it?" Constance leaned toward the fan to admire it. "It's pretty, but the decoration is . . . odd, don't you think?"

The fan was lovely and more delicate than Muriel would have chosen for herself, but this had been a rather special gift, arriving at Worth House by special messenger just as they had descended the staircase to leave for the ball. It was a gift from *him*.

"If you will recall"—Susan quickly spoke before Muriel could muster words into a comprehensive order—"when she was younger, Moo had a particular fondness for learning Classics and such."

"That was ages ago." Constance gazed heavenward. "She was quite the bluestocking back then. I'm relieved to know she's outgrown that silliness."

"I think you'll find that she will always retain some interest in that area." Susan, who had spent her childhood with Muriel, knew her friend had always been obsessed with everything Roman. She tried to temper Constance's censure.

"I'm so very sorry for you, Moo. I hope that part of your past will never be discovered."

Constance would need to work much harder if she were to get a rise out of her cousin tonight. Muriel could tolerate almost anything this evening. She'd never felt happier in her entire life, not even when she'd discovered Signore Biondi and he'd accepted her as his new Latin student. Even she had surprised herself with the discovery of her affection for Sherwin. Whether masked by the surge of anger at their first meeting in Town or disguised as a long, cultivated, mutual understanding, she could not deny that their shared interests had existed from the very first time they met.

"Oh, look at the Earl there." There was only one earl who interested Constance. "Quite a court he's holding."

A bevy of young ladies and their mothers surrounded Sherwin on the far side of the room.

"You'd better join them if you have any hope of catching his attention," Susan recommended strongly, just stopping short of physically pushing her.

Constance smoothed her pale yellow skirts and straightened before stepping toward the Earl to join his admirers.

"What chance do you think she has of securing a dance with him?" Susan's question seemed more rhetorical than one for Muriel. "I have no doubt that man dances with only those he wishes."

There had been a few lucky enough to step onto the dance floor with the Earl. As for Muriel, she did not need to be asked.

"Save me a waltz," Sherwin had told her before she left Signore Biondi's that afternoon. Besides the obvious answer that he wished to share a dance with her, as she did with him, if they did not dance, it would cause further speculation they were not getting on. That was very far from the truth, indeed.

Sherwin finished the current set and strode to Muriel's side to claim his dance. He bowed before her, not too low as to hint of any out-of-the-ordinary connection between them, just the usual nervousness, knowing they were on display, and offered her his arm.

"It is not quite time to gather for the next set." Muriel

accepted his escort, placing her hand upon his arm. If she had not accepted his arm, *that* would have caused a scene.

"I cannot wait any longer to share your company." Sherwin would not return to his mother's side. There was nothing more he wanted at this moment than to be near Muriel, pull her into his arms, and kiss her.

"You looked as if you were well occupied. Do you dare ignore all those lovely ladies who wait attendance upon you while you stand by my side? You shall cause a fresh bout of gossip." She peeked at him out of the corner of her eye, just as depicted in her portrait.

"Let them all talk, say whatever they wish. What care I?" Sherwin slid his hand over his waistcoat pocket, savoring his treasure. "You are the loveliest lady in this room. I cannot tell you how difficult it has been not to give in to the temptation to gaze in your direction. I'd much rather admire you instead of pretending that any of these other . . . *charming* ladies have a remote chance of holding my interest."

"I am sorry you must endure such torture." Muriel dared to laugh at his discomfort.

"I will not endure it for much longer. We may take a turn about the room, or the gallery, or the gardens—anywhere that we might be alone until it is time for the next set."

"You know we cannot be alone—it is most improper," she scolded him.

"Even though we are eng—"

Muriel shushed him and brought the tip of her fan to her lips. "Do not make this any more difficult than it already is, I beg you."

"Very well." He chuckled. "I shan't tease you again."

"I will ask one favor of you, if I may." Muriel stared up at him. "Constance has been forever wishing your attention. Would you do the honor of dancing with her?"

"I only do so because you ask, and I am in a precarious position where I can deny you nothing." Sherwin doubted there was a finer night that this. "And will it break her heart when she discovers I am to wed her cousin?"

"I cannot say, but she will have the pleasure of dancing with you once." Muriel smiled up at him, and Sherwin thought he would lose his solid form and be reduced to a puddle at her feet.

"It was my intention to inform my mother of my decision before attending the ball. I have yet to be successful in that regard, but I promise you that after standing up with your cousin, I shall seek out my mother and inform her that I have decided upon a bride. I will contain myself no longer—even you will not be able to stop me."

"As you wish, my lord." Muriel peeked out at him from the corner of her eye again.

"I shall call on you tomorrow and speak to your father. Then there shall be no more secrets." He placed his hand on hers and wished this moment could last forever. How he adored her. How perfect they were for each other. With a gleam in her eyes that, even with his long-sightedness he could perceive, he could see how she, too, adored him.

"I welcome the opportunity to free myself from the duplicity that surrounds me—I will admit some of which is of my own making." Muriel's hold on his arm relaxed as if in anticipation of their future. "Honestly, Sherwin, I do not believe I could keep another single secret."

Sherwin had asked Constance for a dance, which she accepted and seemed to have thoroughly enjoyed. She spent quite a bit of time in conversation with a group of ladies on the far side of the room before returning to Muriel and Susan.

"I must confess, it would not take much for the Earl to win my affection," Constance whispered, nearly out of breath. "It is only that I've heard the most disheartening thing. All is lost, I'm afraid. He is to be married."

"To whom?" Susan, who could not have known it was Muriel, showed genuine surprise.

Muriel would need to tell her soon. Susan was, after all, her dearest friend, and Muriel had not wished to keep such news from her. But she had to until her father and Sherwin's mother approved the match.

"No one knows." Constance sounded quite put out. "It's a secret engagement. And just as I begin making progress with Amhurst . . . it is most dreadful."

Muriel felt her silly smile, the one Susan had chided her about, returning. She dropped her fan open and raised it to hide the lower half of her face.

"I don't know when they're to make the announcement. I do admit, I am most curious to learn who she is. Do not worry, cousin, I am not so angry." Constance glanced toward the Earl as if there might be a clue to his fiancée's identity. "There is nothing for it. If Amhurst is no longer available, I believe I must turn my attention toward Sir Samuel Pruitt."

That's when Susan dropped *her* fan open and brought it close to her face.

After his set with Constance Kimball, Sherwin sought his mother. He approached Lady Amhurst and stood with both hands resting in the small of his back and planned to wait by her side until he received her undivided attention.

"What is it, Amhurst?" she replied in a cool tone at his presence.

"Might I have a private word with you?" He stared at her, making certain she would not put him off again as she had during the drive there earlier that evening. When he had tried to raise the subject, she had silenced him with a wave of her hand, deeming it more important he listen to her on-going list of instructions.

"Excuse us," Lady Amhurst cooed at the guests around her and nodded her head in a gracious manner to her son.

Sherwin led her off to one side of the room where they were sure not to be overheard. He glanced across the room at Muriel, who gently fanned herself. There were no words to express the delight he felt in seeing her with his gift. She was beyond lovely, and he couldn't wait until he had the chance to stand up with her a second time.

"I think you will be pleased with what I have to say, my lady." Sherwin could not help but smile. As much as his mother wished him to marry, she could not be, he decided, any happier than he.

"What is it, Sherwin?" His mother sounded impatient. "Do you not have a dance with Miss Shrope next? Why don't you go find her?"

He faced his mother and announced, "I wish to inform you that I have decided upon a bride." He placed his right hand upon the precious portrait resting in his waistcoat pocket.

The inquisitive gazes of the guests around them grew curious, but Sherwin knew they would need to wait until both families gave their consent before a public announce-ment could be made.

"You have? That is astonishing news!" Lady Amhurst clasped her hands together in delight, or was it in anticipa-tion? "Who is she, pray tell?"

"Lady Muriel Worth," Sherwin whispered. It felt good to say her name out loud. "I have not spoken to her father as of yet. I shall seek an audience with the Duke of Faraday first thing tomorrow."

Lady Amhurst's smile fell from her lips. "No, I will not agree to this match," she said, her voice becoming softer in her attempt to control her anger. "That gel is not suitable."

Sherwin didn't understand—Muriel was perfect! "Her father is the Duke of Faraday, her brother the Earl of Brent, her uncle Baron Kimball, her brother-in-law—"

"Although quite exceptional, I am not speaking of her family connections." Lady Amhurst did not take a breath before continuing, "I will not have her in ours!"

An immediate silence struck the room, and a chill of dread surrounded him at his mother's declaration.

Sherwin turned to face Muriel. Her cheeks had flushed to a raging scarlet. Even though she stood halfway across the room, she was the only one who could have "heard" every hurtful word of Lady Amhurst's.

The sound of Muriel's fan snapping closed echoed through the room. She threw it forcefully to the floor and crushed its delicate ivory sticks beneath her silk dancing slippers before exiting the ballroom.

Muriel stalked out of the ballroom, turned a corner, and continued down the corridor. She swiped the tears burning her eyes and went straight into the ladies' room to remove herself from the unwanted attention of the other guests.

How dare she? That woman had the audacity to declare that Muriel was not welcome in her family?

That hateful, odious woman. Sherwin's mother. The Dowager Countess of Amhurst.

And what had been Sherwin's reply? Nothing.

She hadn't waited long to see his answer, true, but it had been enough time to know he would remain silent. If Sherwin did not oppose his mother in this, there would be no peace in the future. This was not to be borne. There would be no future for them, Muriel vowed, if he did not stand up for her now.

"Moo, what is it? What has happened that you—" Susan hurried in. Apparently she had followed the swiftly moving Muriel out of the ballroom and had finally caught up to her. "You are . . . oh, goodness—Moo, you are crying."

Nothing had ever made Muriel cry. Until this happened. To be clear, it wasn't Lady Amhurst's rejection . . . it was Sherwin's apparent inability to disagree with his mother.

"What can be so horrible?" Susan rubbed Muriel's arm and took up her gloved hand. "This cannot be. Tell me what I must do for you, dearest."

There was nothing Susan could do.

Muriel pulled free from her friend. "I will be fine, Sukey. Pray you, give me a moment to collect myself." She sniffed and pressed her cheeks with the palms of her hands and squeezed her eyes closed, attempting to calm herself and regain self-control.

"I cannot imagine what happened. One moment you were standing next to me, and the next . . . well, you were dashing out of the room—and you know very well I cannot keep up with you when you run." Susan now took the time to check her own dress and smooth her hair with her hands.

"I am sorry, Sukey. I was not running away from you," Muriel replied, never giving any thought to those who were around her. "It was nothing you did or said, believe me."

Two women approached, chattering loudly in alarm.

"My dear." Mrs. Wilbanks cooed and soothed Muriel by rubbing her shoulders. "Oh, my dear, you are so over-wrought." Turning to Aunt Penny, she said, "She is excessively fatigued. Did I not tell you, Mrs. Parker? Our dear

Muriel has such a delicate constitution, and we have pushed her far too hard. Only see what our insistence that she attend parties every evening has done to her."

"I cannot say what has unsettled you so, but I fear Mrs. Wilbanks is right." Aunt Penny soon stood on Muriel's other side. "I think it best we return home."

"Yes, Aunt Penny, I do not feel well at all." Muriel drew in a ragged breath and feigned a bit of weakness. She did not feel light-headed or tired; she just wanted to leave the premises as soon as it was possible.

The two older women found a place where Muriel could rest and eased her onto a small sofa.

"Retrieve my vinaigrette bottle at once!" Mrs. Wilbanks sent her daughter on the errand with a wave.

No burned feathers, smelling salts, or vinaigrette were going to drive away what ailed Muriel.

Susan returned in a matter of moments and handed a small bottle to Aunt Penny, who lifted the lid and waved it under Muriel's nose.

"You remain with Muriel, Mrs. Parker. We shall retrieve our outer garments and call for the carriage." Mrs. Wilbanks drew Susan away with her to attend to the tasks.

"Oh, no—please, Aunt Penny, I beg of you." Muriel pushed her aunt's hand away. Her eyes watered again, this time from the unpleasant odor. "I shall not swoon."

Susan and Mrs. Wilbanks soon returned with the cloaks. "I asked that the carriage be brought around to the side door so as not to cause a scene."

"That was well done of you, Mrs. Wilbanks." Aunt Penny stood, donned her cloak, then returned to her niece, wrapping the garment around her shoulders and fastening it under her chin. "Do you think you are able to stand?"

Muriel nodded. She stood with her aunt on one side and

Susan on the other. Inquisitive glances and prolonged gazes from some of the female guests followed her departure out the side door.

She reassured herself that no one could know the real reason she felt ill this evening. Continuing forward under the comforting wing of her aunt, Muriel did not look back. She had quite decided that she would never attend another ball, never return to London, and never, ever see Sherwin, the Earl of Amhurst, again.

Chapter Eleven

Muriel had gone before Sherwin had a chance to speak to her, to explain that he had every intention of revisiting their attachment, and their subsequent engagement, with his mother. He ran out of the room on Muriel's trail, only to be barred from entering the ladies' room.

He felt awkward lingering about the door, watching ladies entering and exiting. They giggled and blushed when they saw him—or perhaps it was not him specifically but any gentleman who dare to remain near the females-only area. But he would not leave until he saw her. He waited and waited until one of the ladies' maids informed him that Muriel and her party had left the Burnette residence.

Angry with Lady Amhurst, and angrier still that he could not make amends with Muriel, Sherwin sent for his carriage. He debated the prudence of following Muriel to Worth House and decided he might better consult Freddie in the morning. Sherwin then returned home. His mother would answer for the trouble she had caused.

A sleepless night followed, which prevented him from

further nightmares of the disturbing scene with his mother. But that did not stop him from thinking of it and the actions he must take to set matters between them to rights.

"Put it away, Lewis, all of it," Sherwin ordered the next day upon waking. He would not allow the valet to dictate what he should wear, no matter if the instructions had come from Lady Amhurst.

He did not need to repeat himself. Within five minutes, Sherwin stood in the striped ivory-colored silk waistcoat, buff trousers, and Hessians he'd requested. Lewis gave the brass buttons of the new blue Weston jacket a final polish before holding it out for his lordship.

Sherwin stood by his bureau. He fastened his lover's eye onto a fob and slid it into his left pocket, then placed his gold pocket watch in the other. Ignoring the quizzing glass, which would have been his mother's preference, he motioned for his jacket.

Lewis helped Sherwin don the final garment and stepped back. "Will that be all, sir?"

Turning to the full-length mirror, Sherwin gauged his appearance. "My spectacles, if you please."

"But—I, sir, her ladyship . . . she did not—" Lewis' nervous fluster caused him to stagger backward.

Without a word, Sherwin moved his gaze from the mirror to the valet, commanding the respect he had not previously required from the servant.

Lewis scuttled out of the bedchamber into the dressing room and returned in a matter of seconds. In his outstretched hand he offered Sherwin the pair of wire-rimmed spectacles and intoned, "Your lordship."

For the first time, Sherwin entered the breakfast parlor without a book tucked under his arm. He stepped through the open door and stopped. His mother sat at the far end, near the window.

She said nothing, but the slight arch of her eyebrows indicated her disapproval of his spectacles, retrieved without her permission, his clothes, none of which she had chosen or purchased, and finally, him. He had the uncomfortable feeling that there would be no pleasing her this day.

"Good day, madam." He greeted her with a nod.

"Will you not join me?" Lady Amhurst's unexpectedly sweet tone was one he did not care for. "We shall have the discussion you desire, but I wish that you please be seated." She gestured toward his usual place at the table.

Sherwin entered and moved to where she had indicated. He flipped the tails of his jacket from behind him and settled into the chair.

"Molly," Lady Amhurst called to the kitchen maid. "A plate of buttered eggs and coffee for his lordship."

"Lady Muriel is my choice," he informed his maternal parent.

"I do regret my reaction last night." Lady Amhurst straightened in her seat. "I must admit, you caught me by surprise. I only wish to know if you are quite sure of your decision."

The discussion paused when Molly entered and set a cup of coffee and a plate of eggs before Sherwin. Once the maid left, his mother turned to him again.

"Lady Muriel is a near stranger, whereas I have introduced you to several young ladies I thought you might find of interest. Is there none of them who—"

"Those females whom I've been calling upon for the last month?" Sherwin shared absolutely nothing with them—no interests, no decent conversation. They had no mind, no opinions, no thought other than . . . "Dresses and hats—

female fripperies. They are all thoroughly accommodating, I am sure, and, quite simply, I find them vapid." He sipped from his coffee cup but found his appetite had vanished.

"Where do you expect a lady should direct her attention? Especially a future countess?" Lady Amhurst remained calm, he thought, unnaturally so. She spoke much slower than she normally did, and Sherwin had the distinct feeling she was biding her time. "I do not wish you to make a decision in haste. I have yet to speak to the gel or to her family. Is there not time for a proper courtship?"

"I beg your pardon, your ladyship." Perhaps he had misjudged his mother. Could she truly be reconsidering her position? She was correct about the slight acquaintance between their families. His years of correspondence with Muriel would need to stay confidential for the time being. Despite Muriel's wish to be done with all her secrets, some needed to remain so, perhaps indefinitely. "We shall, of course, wait an appropriate amount of time before announcing our engagement."

Lady Amhurst paused, seemingly in thought, and sipped from her cup before asking, "So there is no . . . *understanding* between the two of you?"

"Not an understanding as much as an expectation. We hadn't anticipated your refusal." Sherwin raised his cup as if he might hide from embarrassment behind it, knowing that what he said was a lie to placate his mother. He and Muriel were resolutely attached. Warmth flushed his face, heating his cheeks.

"I do apologize. It was an overreaction on my part." Lady Amhurst sighed and seemed more relaxed. "Only allow me to think on this, to grow accustomed to the idea."

"I beg your pardon, ma'am." Sherwin blinked his heavy lids. He had not considered that his mother might take the

news of his decision badly, and it explained her violent outburst. He tugged at his cravat; the confounded thing was
strangling him.

"Your announcement was quite unexpected and caught me
unaware. I cannot say, however, I am entirely displeased." She
stood with her cup and saucer in hand.

"Of course we want both families to accept our m-match,
but we would not wish to—to wait m-much . . ." Sherwin
couldn't find the words to complete his statement. He was
finding it increasingly difficult to hold his head upright; it
wobbled from left, right, forward, and back, and it suddenly
seemed impossible to keep his eyes open. With a thud, Sherwin felt the hard surface of the table press against the side of
his face.

"Do not concern yourself, Sherwin." Lady Amhurst's voice
sounded very far away, followed by the crisp *clink* of her
cup settling on the saucer. "I am quite certain all will work
itself out in the end—just as I planned."

That was the last he heard before the blackness envel-
oped him.

Muriel hadn't slept all night. Rising from her bed at day-
break, as was usual, she could no more concentrate on her
morning studies than slumber.

Lady Amhurst's declaration that she would not welcome
Muriel into her family had hurt Muriel more than she could
ever have imagined. The guests had heard the Countess rant
but knew not what or who had caused her rage. Muriel supposed her disgrace might have been complete if it were known
to everyone she was the unacceptable party.

It was a horrible thought.

Muriel rang for Lydia just after ten to dress and headed
below stairs, where she sat before an empty plate in the

breakfast room with a cup of chocolate she kept hold of, just off the saucer.

Perhaps Muriel wouldn't have felt as hurt if Sherwin had instantly stood up for her and for himself, defying his mother. He had every right to, Muriel told herself. After all, he was the new earl, not merely a son. Why could he not marry the woman of his own choosing?

But she strongly feared he would not act against his mother. He and she had both lost so much, after all: husband, sons, brothers. Still, Sherwin had seemed so certain of his mother's support; the question remained, why had the woman reacted so strongly against Muriel?

She heard the footfalls approaching and looked up to see her brother standing in the doorway, wearing his gloves with his hat in hand.

"Where have you been at this hour? Or are you about to leave?" Muriel was in no mood to involve herself in verbal sparring this early in the morning, no matter how Freddie wished to goad her.

"Moo, I'm relieved to find you up." He rushed to her side, drew out a chair, and settled next to her, perching on the edge of the seat. "I am sorry to be the bearer of such alarming news, but I feel you must know."

Muriel somehow dreaded to hear what he had to say. It had to be something terrible for him to appear so distressed. Her anxiety grew, sprouting, perhaps, from the deep sorrow she already felt.

"I've just come from Lloyd Place . . ." Sherwin's London residence. "He's gone."

"Gone?" The china cup she'd been holding dropped onto its saucer, and the chocolate sloshed over the edge onto her fingertips.

"You must be the strong sister I know you to be." Freddie

steadied her forearm with a gloved hand. "They've closed up the house and left Town with no indication of their destination."

Muriel pressed the napkin around her wet fingers and closed her eyes, squeezing them tightly. Sherwin could not leave her—would not, she felt certain. She could not think of what might have happened.

"I know how deeply he cares for you, and of his intention to marry you."

At her brother's admission, she straightened, wide-eyed, and faced him. "How could you know?"

"He told me of his intentions yesterday and asked for my help as to where he might find a certain gift for you."

Her beautiful fan. What a fool she had been to discard it.

"I cannot think he left of his own volition." Freddie's anxious expression was one Muriel did not recognize. "I fear something is amiss here. And from my limited exposure to his parent, I deem his mother . . . domineering. Perhaps it would not be out of the question that she would behave in a rash and unexpected manner."

"Last night Sherwin told her we wished to be married. I'm afraid she did not take it well." Muriel pushed away from the table in a sudden feeling of restlessness, clutching the cloth napkin in her hand. "Actually, Lady Amhurst refused to consider our match."

"Knowing what we do, we cannot remain idle." Freddie sounded angry and took to his feet, as if he were ready to take action.

"I am not in the position of calling the Runners to find him, nor are you, without raising unwanted attention." Muriel set the napkin aside and stood. Never had she felt so helpless. "You must tell me, what is to be done?"

"Something is very, very wrong." Freddie moved near

her and wrapped his arm around her shoulders. "I do not think we can proceed without giving this a bit more thought. I cannot say what options we have at our disposal."

"We cannot proceed? Do not say so. I am merely a female, as you and Papa have so often reminded me." She turned to her brother with tear-filled eyes. "I cannot stand idle. Until *you* decide there is something to be done, what would you have *me* do, Freddie?"

Loud moaning woke him. Sherwin squeezed his eyes closed in an attempt to bear the pain in his splitting head. He reached to touch his temple and confirmed that, despite what he thought, it remained whole. The moan reverberated again; this time he heard it from the inside.

The sound had come from him.

It took several minutes of lying still before he had the courage to pry open his eyes.

Only one at a time.

He lay upon something soft. His bed? Sherwin struggled to roll to his side and rubbed his face, realizing that his spectacles were missing. How long had he been here? Was he ill?

The last thing he remembered was . . . Nothing. He needed a few more minutes to clear his head and for the pounding to abate.

The turn of a doorknob and creaking of hinges told him that he was about to have a guest.

"Lord Amhurst?" a soft voice called to him. Movement and the rustle of fabric reinforced the presence of a female.

"Who's there?" Raising his head, Sherwin squinted toward the doorway, which did nothing to identify his visitor.

"It is Julia . . . Julia Shrope." She approached, carrying something on a tray, and straightened slightly at the door, latching it behind her with the distinct sound of a key turning in the lock.

"Miss Shrope?" He recalled who she was but could not imagine why, of all people . . . "Does your mother know you're here?"

"Mama is below stairs with Lady Amhurst." Miss Shrope set the tray on a surface. "They sent me to check on you."

Sherwin made to sit up when she neared the bed, which caused him considerable pain.

"How are you feeling?" Her kind words and soft touch did much to calm him, although the pain persisted. "You've been drugged. Laudanum, I think. Here, drink this. I'm told it will make you feel better." She held out the glass, and he hesitated before bringing it to his lips.

Sherwin was willing to give it a try. He sipped at the liquid and choked. "What is that?"

"A bit of brandy." Miss Shrope moved back, reacting at once to his discomfort.

"No more, I beg you." He did not like it, but after a few minutes his head seemed to clear, and the pain had marginally subsided. Now that he had his eyes cracked open, Sherwin could tell he was not in his room, or any other, at Lloyd Place. "Where am I?"

"Sandstone Abbey, Wiltshire."

The name meant nothing to him. "Wiltshire?" How long had he been asleep?

"More specifically, you are in my brother Grant's room." Miss Shrope continued to watch him.

"Where is Grant?" Sherwin knew nothing about her family and wondered why he lay in this room.

"Away at Eton."

It's where *he* should have been, at school . . . no, not Eton. There was a place more important he needed to be. . . .

Sherwin should have been in London—with Muriel.

"Muriel waits for me." He remembered now. Yet he still was not quite sure what had happened to him.

"Lady Muriel Worth?"

"Yes." Sherwin had the feeling Miss Shrope knew more than she let on. "I must call on her this afternoon. Why am I here?"

"I heard them, our mothers, speak of her. I'm sure they did not think I overheard, but . . ."

"Yes?" Sherwin had worked his way to the edge of the bed and slid one booted foot, then the other, to the floor. "What did they say?"

"They wish us to marry . . . our mothers, that is." Miss Shrope continued to keep her distance from him. "My mother is not so insistent. At least she wasn't until Lady Amhurst convinced her that we should suit."

"Marry?" Sherwin grabbed hold of a bedpost to steady himself.

"Lady Amhurst likes me very well. She's expressed the need to have a malleable daughter-in-law. My mother could not have asked for a better match—oh, la, sir, you are an earl. And she assured her ladyship of my complete coopera-tion." Her voice trailed to almost an inaudible whisper. "They believe we will do well together because we are both easily controlled."

His mother had sunk to a new low. Drugging him was bad enough, and now openly expressing her plan to manip-ulate him and another. "I shall have her sent to the Dower House, at once, upon my return to Marsdon Manor."

"Lady Amhurst has no intention of removing to the Dower House. She intends to remain the mistress of Marsdon Manor," Miss Shrope replied, still reserved in her response. "She made that very clear to my mother."

"I may have been remiss in my duty and inexperienced at wielding my rank . . . I have, however, learned much during my short stay in Town." In large part, he considered, due to the Earl of Brent. Perhaps the Dower House would be too close. A property in or near Scotland might work better for the future home of the Dowager Countess. Someplace far, far from him and Muriel.

Sherwin had learned quite a lot from observing Freddie the past few days in his conduct with the young ladies, peers, tailors, shopkeepers, persons in service positions in various establishments, including those at Lloyd Place, and, most important, Sherwin's mother.

"I believe my mother suspects that I will no longer tolerate her interference." Sherwin would not allow her to manage him or his affairs from this day forward. "That may explain her desperation. Are you willing to go along with this plan of our mothers'?"

"It does not matter what I wish, my lord. I will do as I am bid." Her gaze remained fixed at her feet.

"You would wed against your will?" Why would she allow herself to be pushed into a marriage she did not want?

"I've heard talk of Lady Muriel." She paused and glanced in his direction. "That she's been— It's very wicked of her. Are you the man she has been secretly meeting? Is that why your mother has removed you from Town in this manner?"

He could have laughed. He'd believed the very same unpleasant thought of Muriel at one time. Sherwin tried to look guilty in order to keep Muriel's secret. Why not allow Miss Shrope to believe the tale, especially if it would give her a distasteful impression of him?

"I'm sure there are worse fates than being married to you." She blushed while making her confession. "But I do not see how I could marry you when it is clear you are already in love with Lady Muriel."

Muriel . . . Sherwin didn't like being so far away from her. He knew the deep, heavy feeling inside his chest would not dissipate until he saw her again.

"She is my heart." Sherwin felt the lump in his throat grow larger and found it difficult to swallow. His eyes filled with tears. He had to believe he would be by Muriel's side once again. "I must . . . I need to get back to London as soon as possible."

Chapter Twelve

Go to London? We have just come from there, and it is so very far away." Miss Shrope pressed a hand to her forehead. "It took us a good part of one day and nearly through the night to travel here. We only stopped to change horses."

"No, matter. I must be on my way." Sherwin still held tightly on to the bedpost, unsure of his balance but knowing for certain what he had to do.

"Shall I have a horse saddled?" She turned from him and began to pace. "I do not quite know how I will manage without our mothers learning of it."

"I cannot ride," he confessed. How very lowering it was to admit his inadequacy.

"Prepare a gig for a swift escape, then?"

"I cannot drive." Even with all of Sherwin's education, he began to see the advantage of the more mundane pursuits he had once thought worthless. They now seemed valuable skills, and he regretted that he had not attempted, much less mastered, them. Something, he vowed, he would rectify. "Perhaps it would be best if I did not alert the staff, in any case. As is my situation, it seems they are loyal to only Lady Amhurst. I'm afraid I shall have to walk."

"Walk? Oh, dear." Miss Shrope clasped her hands before her. "You cannot. You haven't gloves or a hat!"

"Nonetheless, I cannot allow that to deter me."

"What will happen when you are discovered missing?" She was quite right to be concerned about that. It was far more important than traveling without a hat.

"I'm sure my mother will make an effort to have me retrieved. I can assure you, I will do my utmost to thwart any attempt at discovery." How Sherwin would manage, he wasn't sure.

"You cannot dash out willy-nilly 'round the countryside; you are certain to be found." Miss Shrope, by her tone, seemed overwrought.

Sherwin stepped away from the four-poster bed. "I expect I have a more pressing problem of escaping the confines of this house. The door to this room is locked, is it not?"

She glanced back, but Sherwin suspected she must have already known that. Hadn't he heard her lock-and-key entry? "I recall how Grant and Douglas, my other brother, would sometimes sneak out at night. They'd climb down the tree after curfew."

Sherwin stepped toward the window and peered out, noting the large brownish-colored object close to the building, which he supposed was the tree. It was not so close that he would think it reachable from his current position, however.

He reached around for his quizzing glass, which it then occurred to him he'd purposely left behind when he'd dressed. Sherwin felt a momentary panic and patted the pocket of his waistcoat, looking for his lover's eye. Its form under his fingertips assured him of its presence.

"After a few hours of terrorizing the countryside, they'd

be back to bed," Miss Shrope mused aloud. "I never joined them, of course. But I did hear of their ill deeds the next morning. I suppose that, in itself, is good reason to send boys away to school."

Sherwin had certainly never caused such problems, and if his brothers had, he had never heard of their exploits.

"Are you thinking of using that escape route?" Her gaze darted to the window.

"I do not see that I have any alternative." Sherwin pushed the sash window upward and leaned toward the opening. He couldn't estimate the distance to the ground, but if Miss Shrope's brothers could manage it, he would do the same.

Sherwin had no idea of his mother's agenda. Surely they would not proceed to Scotland. To have him recite vows over an anvil at Gretna Green could not be what his mother wanted. Lady Amhurst would find an elopement completely unacceptable. Were they on their way to Marsdon Manor, or were they to remain at Sandstone Abbey? A parson might be on his way to the house at that very moment to perform a marriage ceremony.

"What is my direction once I leave the grounds?" he asked Miss Shrope.

She turned to stare out the window, as if it somehow aided her navigation. "Go down the main drive and turn . . ." She tapped the side of her face with her fingertips. "I don't know if it's south or east."

"No matter," Sherwin assured her. "I've no notion of direction. Left or right will suffice."

"Ah—right, then. Turn right. The village lies directly on the road. It's not very far by carriage. I suppose by foot it will seem longer."

Sherwin knew there remained a great chance he would still get lost. He then glanced down at his new footwear.

Descending a tree in his boots would take some skill, probably another one he did not possess. He told himself if Wellington's army could manage with this type of footwear, so could he.

"I'm sure you'll be able to pick up the mail coach at the Dog and Whistle Inn just outside of Weybridge."

"Very well. Then I'll be off." Sherwin was determined to do this. If his accomplishment could be gauged by his sheer resolve, he would succeed.

Miss Shrope blinked at his announcement.

Of course he was afraid. His hands shook when he reached out to take hold of the window jamb. Sherwin steadied them by grasping the frame tightly. He lifted his foot and realized he could not move further, as the shoulders of his jacket held his arms immobile. "One moment." He replaced his foot on the floor and attempted to remove said garment.

"Allow me to help you." Miss Shrope stepped behind him, grabbed the neck of the jacket, and aided him by pulling his arms free of the sleeves.

Her intake of breath upon display of his undress was followed by her quick turn away from him. Miss Shrope's full attention focused on straightening his jacket and folding it over her arm.

"Before I depart, I must make it known that you are all that is kind, and I am sure there will be a gentleman who will value you for yourself. There is no need to coerce anyone into marriage with you." Sherwin cleared his throat, ending the awkward moment, and returned his attention to the window.

Before a second attempt, he unfastened the cloth-covered buttons of his waistcoat for further ease of movement and pulled the fabric away from his torso. His left hand settled on a pocket, assuring him the small portrait rested safely inside, which gave him strength to continue.

"Again." He nodded, alerting Miss Shrope as well as preparing himself.

He lifted his foot and grabbed the sides of the window frame, moved outward in a single effort, and straddled the sill. Although Sherwin's heart pounded in fright, he would not allow his nerves to dictate his actions. There would be no turning back for him.

"There's a shallow ledge under the window where you should be able to gain your footing," Miss Shrope added, and none too soon. In a few moments Sherwin would be out there on that ledge. "Keep close to the building"—her tone grew more urgent—"and move in the direction of the tree. Oh, do be careful."

He felt for the ledge under the window with the toe of one boot, then tested his footing for stability. It *was* narrow. The ridge was probably meant to be a decorative architectural element, not to support defiant males who disobeyed their parents.

He brought his left leg out the window and stood on the ledge, which must have been only an inch or two at the most, with his feet spread wide. Once outside he faced into the bedchamber, and Miss Shrope, who remained trapped inside. Sherwin hoped his actions would not cause her further problems.

Finding handholds by feel, he slid his feet along the narrow ledge toward the tree. Eventually he came close enough to grasp its branches and pulled himself toward the center, holding on for dear life.

The perilous journey was made even more challenging by his shaking legs, compromising what little balance he had. The boughs strained under his weight, and he realized his next step could be his last.

Sherwin nearly threw himself toward the tree's solid center. His cheek pressed into the rough bark, and an earthy scent filled his nostrils. His hands did not meet when he wrapped his trembling arms around the trunk.

He clung there, catching his breath and calming his frayed nerves. A minute later, he stepped down to the heavier limbs of the lower branches as if he were descending a library ladder. Reaching the last, lowest branch, Sherwin dropped safely to the ground.

He brushed his hands off, making a cursory assessment of his person.

Miss Shrope stood at the window from whence he had come, gazing down at him. "Well done!" she whispered.

Sherwin raised his hands to her. "My jacket, if you please."

She disappeared inside and returned moments later with his blue garment. She held it out the window and released it.

Sherwin easily caught his jacket as it fell. He waved farewell to Miss Shrope, who returned his gesture with a "Good luck to you, my lord."

To Muriel's great relief, Aunt Penny had sent their regrets to Lord and Lady Emerson that they would not be attending the soiree that evening, even before the callers arrived at Worth House that afternoon. Both aunts, Penny and Mary, were concerned with their niece's growing fatigue and deemed quiet and more rest was in order. They were making a concentrated effort to limit her parties for the next week or two and to watch for Muriel's improvement.

It suited Muriel very well.

She was in no mood to pretend that she enjoyed herself

when all she could think of was Sherwin and his safety, for by now, without word of him, she had become convinced he was in some sort of danger. With his disappearance, she became irritable and wholly disagreeable. All of which was explained by Aunt Penny as fatigue and overexertion from the breathtaking pace of the current Season's activities.

The dark circles that rimmed Muriel's eyes might have been initiated by her early-morning studies. They grew more pronounced with her sleeplessness over Sherwin's well-being.

She had never felt more helpless, or more angry at Freddie for not coming to her aid. He was a man, or so it seemed; why could he not do something? And Muriel wondered if there was truly nothing she could do to help locate Sherwin.

"What do you think of that, Lady Muriel?" Lord Peter, who had made a pest of himself of late, insisted on an answer. "Lord Amhurst absconding to Gretna."

"There's no need for an elopement, I think. He's got a special license, to be sure," Sir Calvin corrected his friend.

"All right, then. Whom, out of all his ardent admirers, did he choose, do you think?" Mr. Stanley looked about him to hear the proposed candidates.

"I am sure I cannot say." Mr. Ambrose turned to Muriel. "What say you, my lady?"

"I have no idea," she replied rather coolly. "You might want to check the betting book at White's. I hear that's where all the important wagers are registered."

Lord Peter, Mr. Ambrose, Mr. Stanley, and Sir Calvin all laughed.

"And how on Earth would you have knowledge of the betting book at White's?" Mr. Ambrose, who sat with Sir Calvin and Mr. Stanley between him and his rival, Lord Peter, seemed amazed that Muriel was in possession of a brain.

What would Mr. Ambrose's opinion be of Muriel when he discovered she was capable of thought as well? Men! She could not tolerate their company any longer—she wanted nothing more to do with them. Farewell and good riddance too!

Muriel wondered if she might impose upon Sir Samuel again. Perhaps there was something he could do, unlike Freddie, to help locate Sherwin. Sir Samuel, she considered, was far cleverer than her own flesh and blood.

"Moo!" Susan nudged her. "We have new visitors, and these gentlemen are about to leave."

Muriel pushed aside her thoughts of Sir Samuel and turned to bid the gentlemen farewell.

"Lady Muriel . . ." Sir Calvin remained behind. "Might you accompany me for a drive in the Park tomorrow?"

She could not, in all good conscience, pass any time in his, or any other gentleman's, company, when she did not know of Sherwin's fate.

"I am sorry. I am occupied tomorrow afternoon." Muriel would make sure she was, for his benefit. She recognized Sir Samuel's voice; he must have been just entering Worth House. "Perhaps another time, Sir Calvin?"

Sir Calvin bowed. "I shall inquire when next we meet and hope for better luck."

Had she learned nothing from spouting untruths? Muriel drew Susan close by her arm. "Pray find Sir Samuel and tell him he is to accompany us for a drive in the Park tomorrow."

"Us? Whatever are you—" Susan leaned against the firm insistence of Muriel's hand, pressing her forward.

"And if you come across Freddie," Muriel added, "inform him that he will also be joining us."

"Sometimes I think you go too far, Moo," Susan replied over her shoulder.

"I am certain you are correct, Sukey. I promise I shall reform my ways." But now was not the time.

Sherwin located the village of Weybridge within an hour's time. He bypassed the main street, thinking he would not be noticed, keeping a careful watch, thankfully at a distance, for the Dog and Whistle Inn. He approached the establishment and stepped inside, not quite knowing what to expect.

"Might I inquire as to when the coach leaves for London?" Sherwin could see but not read the signboard on the wall, which perhaps held some information.

"Lunnun, you say?" The man in a brown jacket behind the counter leaned closer to Sherwin, which made him more unrecognizable.

Without his hat, cane, and gloves, Sherwin felt woefully underdressed to command any amount of authority or respect from anyone.

"If I may introduce meself, milord? Rodney James, proprietor and manager of the Dog 'n' Whistle, at your service. The mail coach don't arrive until after four, and don't 'spect it ta leave fer near six or so hours yet."

"Oh, I see." Sherwin wasn't sure what he would do until the coach arrived or until its departure.

"There be a private parlor ready if'n yer lordship is in need of a place ta rest or 'ave a meal whiles ya wait."

"Yes, that sounds splendid." If nothing else, it would keep Sherwin out of sight. Might he mention to Mr. James to remain silent if anyone should ask about him? Sherwin decided against it. His request might draw more attention his way.

He said nothing and followed Mr. James up the staircase to a private parlor. Sherwin remained there for nearly seven hours. He spent his time waiting, sitting quietly, pacing a bit, sipping tea, and nibbling on bread and cheese throughout the afternoon.

At a knock on the door, Mr. James entered with a servant girl, who piled the empty dishes on her tray.

"The mail coach is 'ere," Mr. James told him. "I fought ya might want to settle yer accounts 'bout now."

"My 'accounts'?" Sherwin stood and had the most uncomfortable feeling. "I beg your pardon, sir. What exactly . . ."

"Payin' fer coach passage, fer one thing. An' what's 'bout the parlor, a private one at that—it costs aplenty—and yer meal?" Mr. James had lost his prior friendly manner of address. "Yer fancy city wardrobe musta been dear. Are tellin' me you ain't got the blunt?"

Money. He was asking to be paid. Mr. James had every right, of course. But Sherwin hadn't a farthing with him.

"Don't thinks I don't know?" He stared hard at Sherwin with one squinting eye. "A swell the likes of you, showin' up 'ere, lookin' like ya do? Wiffout a hat? No travelin' coat? Ya smell of a lad in trouble."

Sherwin gulped, finding it difficult to swallow.

"And whens a couple o' fellows come 'round asking for a chap wif yer looks, Roddy, I says to meself"—he poked his own chest, as if he truly were in conversation—"I ain't givin' the lad upstairs away. 'E might be in the briars, but he ain't done nuffin' bad. No, I says. So I turns 'em away. Says I ain't never seen ya."

"I've done nothing wrong," Sherwin explained. Mr. James may not have had a formal education, but he clearly knew exactly what Sherwin was all about.

"And this is 'ow ya repays me fer savin' yer hide?" Mr. James balled his hands into fists.

"If I could only . . ."

Even without his glasses, Sherwin could see Mr. James'

head angled downward, examining the London-made attire, which must have, if Sherwin had given it some consideration, been costly, indeed. At the time he hadn't given a thought as to the bill; Freddie had taken care of the details.

"I had—have no intention of leaving without paying. It's only that . . ." Sherwin wasn't exactly sure what he was going to do. Perhaps Mr. James had a suggestion? "I haven't any money with me."

"Well, now, I 'spose ye gots somethin' of value?" The innkeeper appeared to have found his good humor, and a wide smile returned to his face. "A trade's what we'll do ta settle yer accounts."

The most precious item Sherwin possessed was his lover's eye, and he could not part with that. His hand slid protectively over the pocket where it rested.

"Oh, no, not there—I be wantin' yer pocket watch. 's gold, I take it?"

Sherwin drew his watch into his palm, catching the play of the flickering candlelight on the elaborately engraved cover. The timepiece had never been of real use to him . . . until now. "You will take this as payment for my stay in your . . . establishment and for passage in the coach to London?"

"Oh, aye, milord." Mr. James nodded. "And the chain, if ya please. We'll be considerin' that a deal amongst us gentlemen."

"I agree." Sherwin unclipped his small portrait from the bartered item and handed the gold watch, fob, and chain to Mr. James. There it was—payment in full.

Fifteen minutes later he was seventh in line for the mail coach. Sherwin stood behind an old woman clutching a small brown panting object, which he surmised was a dog, in one arm; she had her other wrapped around a young, sickly child.

At the head of the line were two large men and their large wives.

Sherwin turned to take his last glimpse of the Dog and Whistle in the fading light of day. By this time tomorrow he should surely be in London, and if luck were with him, by Muriel's side.

Chapter Thirteen

Muriel sat in the small parlor with a book after supper Tuesday evening. She hadn't actually been reading the book, merely holding it up before her face, pretending, to anyone who might chance to pass in the corridor, that she was engrossed in the pages. Nothing could have been further from the truth.

Both Aunt Penny and Mrs. Wilbanks thought Muriel needed quiet, time to rest. She and her aunt had been out nearly every night since she had arrived in Town. Susan and her mother, once they had arrived in London, had joined them whenever they could. It seemed that Muriel had been busy nearly every hour of every day.

"One evening at home should do you a world of good," Mrs. Wilbanks had told her just before she and Susan had left for their evening's entertainment.

How could Muriel read? How could she do anything while Sherwin's fate remained unknown to her?

Long before she had sat for supper, Muriel had penned a missive to Signore Biondi canceling their Wednesday morning lesson, sending it in the very same prearranged manner she had always contacted the tutor. The young messenger's name was Marcello, and he stopped by twice a day, checking the place where Muriel hid her correspondence.

It was impossible for her to concentrate on her studies. If only there was something Muriel could do to help to find Sherwin.

Two hours later she went to bed. Not that she slept. She would probably look worse than she had the day before. Her aunt and Mrs. Wilbanks would be quite put out, not knowing why Muriel's health continued to decline. She could just imagine the next step would be a tisane or poultice. After that they might send for a physician.

How could Muriel tell them that what she really needed was a Bow Street Runner?

Knowing she would be unable to sit placidly at the breakfast table the next morning, she had a tray brought up to her room but allowed the contents to remain untouched.

After barely touching her toast and tea, Muriel donned a frock for her drive in the Park with Susan, Freddie, and Sir Samuel later that afternoon. If she could manage to have a private word with Sir Samuel and explain her—Sherwin's—predicament, perhaps he would come to her aid once again.

Muriel descended the stairs, still deeply disappointed at her brother's inability to act when action was clearly needed. She turned right, heading for the foyer.

A cacophony of male laughter echoed down the corridor. She identified her father as one of the participants, but the identity of the other gentleman remained a mystery.

Moving cautiously and quietly toward her father's library, she leaned around the corner to observe. Muriel felt uneasy at the jovial scene before her. The Duke and Sir Samuel stood at the doorway, shaking hands, as if sealing a business deal.

"What are you doing? What's—" Freddie approached, coming from behind her.

Muriel straightened and gasped in fright. She waved, shushing him, and returned to her post, leaning around the corner to catch a glimpse.

Freddie stepped lightly, nearing with care, and peered around the corner just above his sister's head.

"No father could ask for a better prospect than you," said the Duke. "Now, if you can only persuade the young lady to accept. I cannot predict how onerous a task that will be."

"Does he mean *you*?" Freddie's outburst could have given them away, and Muriel shushed him again.

"I will be the first to wish you happy." The Duke leaned toward Sir Samuel and said in a softer voice, "Good luck to you, Samuel, eh?"

"Thank you, Your Grace." Sir Samuel stepped away, moving toward the marbled foyer, in Muriel and Freddie's direction. "I am to accompany her to the Park soon. I certainly hope I will manage to approach the subject with some sort of poise. I must confess, I feel as if I'll make a muddle of the whole thing."

"I'm sure you'll manage just fine," the Duke replied. "There isn't a gentleman alive who feels confident in such matters."

Muriel stepped back, urging her brother to retreat around the corner. She led him through the parlor, then up the staircase to her bedchamber to make certain their conversation would not be overheard.

"That cannot mean Sir Samuel is about to propose, can it?" Muriel could not imagine how this had come about. How had his commonplace regard for her taken a warmer turn?

"He dashed well is about to offer for someone. When

Father is that jubilant about Sir Samuel coming up to scratch, whom do you think it could be?" Freddie carried on in an animated fashion. "Common sense tells me it might be you."

"Since when do you have any sense? Samuel has no intention of making me an offer." Muriel strode past her dressing table to her bookcase. "No. No. It cannot be true."

Sir Samuel had no notion of Muriel's affection for Sherwin. How could he? She had only recently come to the realization herself. In the past she had relied on Sir Samuel to aid her. Had he understood her trust in him as romantic interest?

"But why?" She uttered the words on a sigh to herself. "How should he ever think to offer for me? No, I simply cannot believe it."

"Has Sir Samuel hinted at his affection?" Freddie paced to the end of the room.

"No, never." Muriel no longer felt comfortable asking Sir Samuel for help locating Sherwin.

She drew *Tragedies of Sophocles* from the bookcase and allowed it to fall open, revealing the iron key and folded map Sir Samuel had given her. Muriel wondered if she had misinterpreted his intentions. She hadn't thought so, but it seemed she might have been wrong.

"So this is where you are hiding!" Sir Samuel appeared at the doorway of Muriel's bedchamber. "I beg your pardon, but His Grace instructed me to locate you, Brent."

"Right. Sorry to keep you waiting, ol' man." Freddie moved to exit but turned back to address his sister. "You ready to join us, Moo?"

Muriel glanced from the open book and its contents before closing the tome and pushing it back into its place in the bookcase. If asking Sir Samuel to help her attend her private lessons had resulted in a marriage proposal, she could not imagine what asking him to help locate Sherwin would bring.

He'd been in the coach for hours on end. Sherwin endured the discomforts of the hard seats and cramped interior. The experience was made worse by Mr. Goodwin's uncanny ability to slumber in this most uncomfortable circumstance. His head rested upon Sherwin's shoulder, lolling about, and Mr. Franks, on the right, pinned his arm to his side. The snores and coughing of Sally, the child, and her guardian, Miss Phelps, added a feminine aspect to the interior quartet. The blare of the horn before every stop and, it seemed, at every intersection was the highlight of the journey.

He hadn't expected that the pocket watch he'd traded in exchange for his passage might have been of any help to tell him how many hours had passed. There'd been many stops, most where the passengers barely had time to stretch their legs, and once they'd been supplied with a bite to eat before returning to the confines of the coach.

The vehicle listed and rattled to a stop again. They were about to disembark for another change of horses. The door swung open, and the driver called out, "End o' the line— Lunnun."

After everyone had exited, Sherwin moved forward in his seat, readying himself to disembark. *End of the line?* This was it: they had arrived in London!

Never had he experienced so treacherous a journey in a wheeled vehicle. Was it his imagination, or had this last leg been more gravity-defying than the earlier parts of the trip? At times he felt as if they'd gone airborne.

He gripped the side of the coach and stepped outside. Sherwin peered around at his surroundings. This was London? It was not any part of the city he recognized. "Where, exactly, are we?"

"Town's right there, ya see, yonder." The man stabbed his large finger to the left, down the road.

Had Sherwin expected they'd deliver him to the doorstep of Lloyd Place? Perhaps if they had stopped at the gates of Hyde Park . . . that was a place he recognized . . . only one of very few. "How am I to get to . . ." He stared at the driver.

"Don't rightly know, gov. S'pose you can hire yourself a hack." He slammed the door closed. Then he clarified, "A hackney cab. Just down the way there." The man pointed somewhere behind Sherwin.

"A hackney?" he repeated. It had cost him his gold watch to get this far. Sherwin didn't know what he had left that was worth trading. His hand stole over his waistcoat pocket.

If he could engage a hackney cab, where would he go? He wanted to rush to Muriel at Worth House, except he could not be presented in his current disheveled state.

He knew barely a soul in Town—a handful of casual social acquaintances, no one he could turn to for help. Then it came to him—a man who had always, without question, lent him support: Signore Biondi.

With his destination set, Sherwin gazed across the road. There, several coaches stood idle, ones, he thought, meant for hire. How to do so without money was another matter, but he did not despair. He had made it this far on his wits and his pocket watch, he would manage to see himself the rest of the way to Town.

He put himself in mind that he was an earl and would try to conduct himself in a noble manner. Most of all he imagined the Earl of Brent and exactly how he would behave in a situation such as this.

"Excuse me, my man," he addressed an idle, beefy chap sitting upon the box of his rig. "By any chance are you—"

"Off wiff ye, ya toff!" the man rumbled back without the benefit of hearing Sherwin's request, shaking a beefy fist at him. "Yer a beggar, that be certain. I'll have none of ya."

Sherwin staggered back, fairly fearing for his life. This was badly done of him. How would he manage to—

"'Ere, look, gov. Yer going about it the wrong way," the driver called out to him, waving Sherwin back in his direction.

Sherwin returned to the mail driver, who met him halfway. "Did you not say I could hire a hack—" He pointed in the same direction the driver had previously.

"Lookie, here. I can sees yer havin' a bit o' difficulty." The driver winked and pulled on Sherwin's sleeve. Only hard enough to urge him in the opposite direction. "Allow me to be of assistance. You come wiff me, now, lad."

"I would sincerely appreciate that, sir." Sherwin nodded, following along amicably.

"I can sees ye've gots yourselfs in a bit of a bind, and I don't wants to sees ya dig yerself in any deeper. I can sees yer a good lad at heart."

"Why, thank you, sir." Sherwin continued, "I am having some difficulty at the moment, and it would be kind of you to lend me a hand. I assure you, it will not be forgotten."

"Then just remember my name. Georgie. Ol' Georgie Hope."

"Really?" Sherwin could hardly believe his luck. "I shall remember you, Mr. Hope, and I assure you, when my circumstances are . . . better, I shall."

"Oh, aye, ye do that, lad." Mr. Hope chuckled as if he would grow older and grayer before he'd ever see his kindness returned.

They walked about halfway down the block, bypassing a good several vehicles standing idle. Sherwin's surrounds appeared mostly gray. The buildings did not appear as ornate, and the streets were not as clean as the London to which he'd recently become accustomed.

"Look alive, Danny!" The driver called out. "This 'ere's my pal, Mr. Turner.

"I think the two of you gentlemen can work out the rest by yourselves, eh?" The driver winked at Sherwin again and gave him a resounding clap on the back.

"Th-thank you, Mr. Hope." Sherwin vowed he would remember the driver who had helped him on the next step to finding Muriel. He looked to the man sitting on the box. "I need a ride to Number 4 Tavistock Road."

Mr. Turner wore a dark, ratty coat and tilted his head. "It'll cost you, gov," he said in a voice that sounded as rough as the ride Sherwin had just survived.

"I have no money." He said it right up front. Sherwin would not be humiliated as he had been at the Dog and Whistle at his inability to pay his way.

"Well, let's see . . ." Mr. Turner scratched his whisker-stubbled jaw and eyed Sherwin. "Seein' ye've been highly recommended, so to speak, I s'pose we can makes ourselves some sort of deal, wot?"

"I find that agreeable, sir." Sherwin didn't have any other choice. He had no doubt Freddie, the Earl of Brent, could forge a deal on a promise and a handsome smile.

"That's a nice jacket I sees." Mr. Turner motioned for Sherwin to turn about and display his garment. "Wouldn't be work of Weston, would it?"

"Why, yes, it is." If handing over his jacket would be enough to see him safely to Signore Biondi's, then so be it. It appeared that he and the driver understood each other quite well. "If you would be so good as to lend me a hand, kind sir?" He would need Mr. Turner's help to strip the garment off his back. Sherwin began to undo his brass buttons to rid himself of his new jacket and pay his passage.

Muriel sat next to Susan, across from Sir Samuel, on the drive to Hyde Park in the open-air coach. Never had she felt so nervous in his company. He didn't exactly appear the study of tranquility himself. Muriel exchanged a few quick glances with Freddie, who sat to Sir Samuel's left, knowing he was privy to the goings-on in their father's library a scant hour ago. Did her brother notice the addled manner of their male companion?

Susan seemed the only serene one of the four, gazing at the passing scenery. She wore a lemon yellow and white dress and a Capucine-colored Spencer that matched her new bonnet, the one that Muriel had borrowed the other day.

They rounded the corner, passing through the gates of Hyde Park, joining the long string of carriages.

"What say we pull over and take a stroll?" Freddie suggested.

"I suppose that would be all right." Susan turned to the left. "Moo? Sir Samuel?"

"Why not?" Muriel replied without really caring. As long as she wasn't left alone with Sir Samuel. She felt horrible that she had such thoughts about her friend.

"Sounds splendid!" Sir Samuel exclaimed, rather a bit too brightly.

The carriage pulled out of the queue, coming to a halt just to the side. Freddie disembarked first, followed by Sir Samuel. It seemed to Muriel that the gentlemen took an extraordinarily long amount of time dawdling and glancing about before turning back to the coach. Freddie took hold of Muriel's, then Susan's, hands, helping the ladies step to the ground.

"Lady Muriel." Sir Samuel did not waste a second and offered his arm to escort her.

"Thank you, Sir Samuel." What else could she say? A part of her felt hesitant about walking alone with him, even though her brother and her friend were only a few feet behind them.

"Miss Wilbanks"—Freddie then followed by example— "I would be honored."

Off to the left, the string of carriages out for a drive stretched far beyond where Muriel could see. She and Sir Samuel bid oncoming pairs of strollers a good day with slow nods of their heads while they passed.

Sir Samuel seemed to fidget so. He stretched the fingers of both hands and repeatedly tugged at his gloves in such a manner that Muriel thought he should quite ruin them. He repeatedly cleared his throat, as if he was about to say something, but he remained silent.

Never had Muriel been so grateful for her bonnet. If she kept facing straight ahead, she would not meet Sir Samuel's gaze. So keen was her discomfort, she thought he must have sensed it through her gloved hand resting upon his.

The mood between them felt very odd, whereas before they had had no difficulty when they spoke, and conversation came without effort. It seemed now neither of them had anything to say, and the silence stretched on.

How unfortunate this was. Muriel had always held Sir Samuel in the highest regard. Why, oh why, did he harbor more affection for her than she for him? It ruined all manner of ease between them.

"I had meant to ask you about your impression of my cousin." Muriel wondered, if only just slightly, how far

Constance had proceeded with her plan of snaring Sir Samuel. And could he have any knowledge of it?

"Miss Kimball?" There was an unmistakable lightening of his tone at the mention of her name, if only slight. "Oh, yes. We have had several conversations. I find her very agreeable, and there is more than a passing resemblance between the two of you. Your mothers were sisters, were they not?"

"Yes, that's correct." Muriel wasn't sure if his reply was a compliment or not.

"Both celebrated beauties in their day, I hear. Lady Kimball is still a handsome woman, as is Mrs. Parker." Sir Samuel seemed to consider his words. "I do wish I had met your mother. They say she was the most beautiful of the three."

"Have you not seen her portrait at Faraday Hall?"

"Yes, but your sisters tell me it does not do Her Grace justice."

Muriel could not say. All she had was the portrait. She barely remembered her mother at all.

"Returning to the topic of Miss Kimball, I need to tell you that I have had the pleasure of standing up with her on more than one occasion." Sir Samuel suddenly became quite animated now that they began to converse about Constance. "She is a very fine dancer. I do not know if I have ever seen anyone more graceful upon the dance floor, and her form is—" He quickened his pace down the path, and Muriel had some difficulty keeping up with him.

"Please, Sir Samuel—you walk too fast."

"I beg your pardon." Slowing to their previous tempo, Sir Samuel, with some degree of agitation, continued. "I should not be discussing such matters with you. It is indelicate."

Muriel turned her head in such a way as to observe him. His cheeks had reddened, and he took a moment to straighten, regaining his composure.

"Suffice it to say, we rub along fairly well together, and tomorrow I have the privilege of taking her out for a drive."

His news of courting came as a surprise to Muriel this time.

"Even though I had not made plans for this afternoon, it happened that an outing was bespoken for me." Now his gaze met hers in the most implicating manner. "Not that I mind in the least."

It was time for Muriel's face to flush. She had to own, she had taken liberties with their friendship. She had treated him as if he were her own kin—worse than that. She had regarded him as no more than a servant, ordering him about, sending him on any task she pleased.

"I suppose you might well be vexed with me." Muriel thought he had every right to be.

"Never fear. You did not compel me to dance with her."

No, she hadn't.

"Nor did you coerce me into any other action."

Muriel had to stare at him again. What did he mean?

"Miss Kimball is . . . how shall I put it? . . . insistent when it comes to making her mind known." The exhale from Sir Samuel seemed to relieve some pressure he appeared to be experiencing, but soon his manner grew tense once more. "I find I cannot deny her. She is, after all, family, your cousin."

Muriel and Sir Samuel drew ahead, and they could speak in a voice not to be overheard by Susan and Freddie. It was something she had dreaded.

"I must confide in you, Lady Muriel," Sir Samuel began.

Oh, dear, must he? She took in a small breath, unsure if it would be possible to exhale.

"I came to Town in the hopes I might find that certain young lady every gentleman seeks." He paused, and Sir

Samuel could have been looking at her for reassurance, but the brim of Muriel's hat shielded her eyes. "This has come upon me quite suddenly. I had no notion of the change in my regard for this certain young lady until recently. No one was more surprised than I to discover that I possessed affection for one with whom I have had a standing acquaintance."

This was what she had dreaded. With every phrase, Sir Samuel might be speaking of her. Muriel did not wish to let on that she knew of his newfound admiration. "Really, you have finally found her?" She had to say something. "How lucky for you! Is it a match, then? May I wish you happy?"

"I do not expect she is aware of my feelings, although we have spent a great deal of time in each other's company, and I have come to realize how much I have grown to care for her." He cleared his throat. "I suppose since we are not acquaintances but friends, I am unsure how to proceed. I would not wish to ruin the companionship we already share. . . ."

"That is sound thinking, if you ask me." Muriel did not wish him to continue, and the sooner she parted company with him, the better. Even if the unpleasant alternative necessitated that she walk with her brother, whom she presently held out of favor. "I shall give this matter some thought. Would you mind walking with Susan for a bit, Sir Samuel? I'd like a word with Freddie." Muriel turned her attention behind her as she and Sir Samuel slowed, ending his conversation altogether and bringing their foursome to a halt.

Chapter Fourteen

I must protest. I have hardly spent any time in your delightful company, Miss Wilbanks." Freddie tipped his hat to Susan. "I have barely had the chance to compliment you on your choice of color and have not had the opportunity to expound on the delights of your bonnet."

"You are an incurable flirt, Freddie. And let it be known, I am quite immune to your charms." Susan waved him away and stepped closer to Sir Samuel.

Freddie gasped as if he were wounded. "I have no ulterior motive, only admiring a lady's wardrobe. I'm sure Sir Samuel will share my opinion of your superb fashion sense."

"Allow me a closer study, if you will." Sir Samuel graciously offered his arm, and they moved forward along the path.

"Ouch!" Freddie winced when Muriel took hold of his arm rather forcefully. "Do take care, will you? Nearly shredded the sleeve, and it's new."

The forest-green jacket fit him exceptionally well. His buff inexpressables gave the illusion his lower limbs were much longer than they actually were. He cut a figure of which any Corinthian would be proud. At the moment, however, Muriel had a rather unladylike opinion of him.

"I do not believe I have remarked on your lovely carriage dress, my dear." Freddie widened his eyes and made a show of amazement regarding Muriel's military-style redingote. "What color is that?"

"It's called Verona blue, and it *is* new." She knew he had no interest in the hue of her garment whatsoever. Muriel did not wish to share his company either. Her simmering anger necessitated that she say something truly horrid to him. "It would look dreadful on you, far too unflattering for your light brown locks."

"The sun tends to fade my hair in the summer, but I vow, I could manage that hue in the winter, when my hair darkens nearly to the color or yours." Freddie slowed their progress, whether from his exertion of verbal sparring with his sibling—which she was under the distinct impression he could manage to do and walk at the same time—or that he had another reason for wanting to lag farther behind Susan and Sir Samuel, Muriel could not be certain.

"Sukey is right: your charms are quite ineffective, and your wits have gone begging!" If her brother thought she should behave in any other than an unkind manner toward him, he was thoroughly mistaken. Muriel was still quite vexed at his refusal to help her find Sherwin.

Lady Maria Greenfield and Mr. Thomas Hollensby, who were at that time passing the siblings, joined Freddie's laughter, which Muriel suspected was not from their finding a shared humor as much as identifying her brother as the joke. It was a sentiment on which she would agree.

"I certainly hope this is not the response I receive from

every female in Town." He'd stopped chuckling and put on a show of mock devastation.

"Lady Maria and I hardly count as *every* female. If you were practiced in simple arithmetic, you could quickly calculate that we are only two."

Freddie's pace slowed further, while Sir Samuel and Susan's lead grew larger. A lull in the oncoming foot traffic gave them a few minutes' privacy.

"Why are we strolling through the Park? Why can we not drive through and be done with the whole wretched business?" Muriel scolded him.

"Because, my dear Moo, you desperately need a distraction. Even though you may consider this task tedious, it removes you from the town house and, for a time, relieves you of some of your constant worry over Amhurst's absence." Freddie spoke without any humorous tone. "It does you no good, Moo. I'm sure the exercise and air cannot harm you in the least."

Her fingers dug into his arm to hold herself upright. The truth in what he said weakened her resolve to display an unwavering facade. The others around her might not have seen any difference in her behavior, but it seemed she hadn't fooled her brother. Muriel didn't know if she could stand on her own any longer. "I do not think I can bear being seen in public. I cannot pretend to enjoy myself, not without knowing that Sherwin— It is a facade I am unable to maintain."

"You must endure, sister." Freddie placed his hand over hers as if the action would lend her strength. "I've thought quite a bit about what you last said to me. So I made a few inquiries and found some men to check into Amhurst's disappearance."

"Oh, thank you, Freddie!" Tears of relief sprang to Muriel's eyes that something was finally being done to locate Sherwin.

"Now, now, no waterworks, please. My ego's taken enough of a blow from you, Sukey, and Lady Maria. Don't let it be known I've done you a kindness. I don't need my reputation to be tarnished as well."

The front door opened at 4 Tavistock Road. The kind soul who had relayed Sherwin to the address had insisted on having his ivory waistcoat as well. Shivering in only his shirt-sleeves, trousers, and boots, Sherwin did not speak but was recognized immediately.

"It's'a me, Giorgio, Mista Lloyd." The servant opened the door wide and welcomed Sherwin inside. He called out to someone, "*Dica il padrone.*"

Sherwin followed Giorgio to the front parlor, where the hearth fire warmed the room, and, truth be told, warmed his worn, travel-weary bones.

"Please, you must sit. Please, sit." Giorgio motioned to a chair near the fire. "The Signore, he *prossimo qui*—soon come now."

"Thank you, Giorgio." As Sherwin moved toward the hearth, he felt the physical as well as emotional toll of his journey weighing heavily upon his shoulders. The relief of being surrounded by something familiar and comforting was welcoming beyond words.

"Ah, *buon*—" Signore Biondi stood at the doorway. His normal jubilant greeting vanished, replaced by an angry tone, "No, no, how is this possible, you arrive here half-naked? Giorgio, go quickly—*prendere il mio abito.*"

The Latin tutor shrugged out of the maroon velvet banyon and slipped it onto Sherwin, drawing it over his shoulders.

Sherwin felt the residual warmth seep into his arms, the outside of his legs, and across his back.

After seeing Sherwin settled comfortably into a chair, Signore Biondi stepped away, poured some dark liquid from an ornately cut glass container into a small glass, and offered it to him. "Drink this, eh?"

Sherwin accepted the glass, though he eyed it suspiciously. He could barely bring himself to swallow the contents. It burned from his throat all the way to his stomach, lending not much comfort, but it managed to warm his insides.

"*Che cosa*—what has happened to you?" Signore Biondi paced the length of the room, stopping for a moment when Giorgio returned with another banyon. This one was identical to the first, except dark blue in color. "Where are your clothes? How do you come to be like this?"

"I did what was needed to return to London—to Muriel—*la Signorina*." Sherwin straightened the fingers of his clenched hand, revealing his lover's eye. "All that matters is that I am here, Signore. I had thought you might help me."

"Of course, of course." Signore Biondi's sympathetic voice soothed and reassured Sherwin that his decision to come there had been the right one.

"I think I need to contact Muriel's brother, the Earl of Brent," Sherwin put forth, his fatigue compromising his ability to reason the obvious.

"At once. Giorgio!" The Signore snapped his fingers.

Paper, quill, and ink arrived upon a small table next to Sherwin's chair. He eagerly took up the quill, dipped it into the ink, and made the first stroke upon the paper, then stopped.

"I cannot see properly to—"

"Ah, yes, *dimenticato*—I forget, *perdona*. I forget, you cannot see. Allow me to write your letter for you." Signore Biondi relieved Sherwin of the inked quill and, with the paper, removed to a writing desk in a corner of the room. "What is it you wish to tell him?"

Sherwin began to dictate, explaining his whereabouts, his circumstance, and asking for Freddie's assistance. Signore Biondi read the missive back to Sherwin, making certain it contained everything the Earl would need to know as well as the urgency of the situation.

Signore Biondi snapped his fingers. "Giorgio, have Marcello deliver this." He handed it to his trusted servant. "Tell him it is to go the same place—he knows where."

Muriel stared into her dressing table mirror and could not believe she would really be returning to Almack's. One week ago Sherwin had stood in the middle of the assembly rooms and called out her name—Moo. Now she had no idea where he was.

"Look at you, Lady Muriel." A very pleased Lydia toyed with one of Muriel's curls, trying to get it to lie just right. "I can't believe you haven't entertained a single offer."

She wouldn't speak of it to her abigail. She might never speak of it again. The mere thought of her lost engagement might bring on a fresh bout of tears.

"These embroidered rosebuds on the pale green gauze overdress match perfectly with the ivory satin gown." Lydia tucked the very same rosebuds into the hair she'd just styled with the hot tongs.

But there was no one Muriel cared about to admire them. She then grieved for her beautiful, delicate fan—the one she'd crushed beneath her silk slipper. It was a silly thought, considering her current concern, but how could she have behaved so childishly?

"You are an absolute vision, Moo." Freddie stood at the doorway to her bedchamber. He cut a fine figure in his evening wear: white waistcoat, knee breeches, clocked stockings, matching black exquisitely tailored jacket, and dancing pumps.

Muriel indeed felt ethereal, as if she had no substance and did not exist at all.

Freddie strolled in, and Lydia dipped a curtsy before leaving the two siblings' company.

"I am glad you will be there with me, Freddie." Muriel stood and took hold of his arm as if it were a lifeline. She wasn't sure how she would survive this night.

He held her hand firmly in his, resisting her efforts to pull free. "I know I have promised to see you through this evening, but I will not be seeing you to Almack's."

"What?" Freddie had betrayed her again. Was he to be forever changing his mind and disappointing her?

He glanced toward the dressing room, making certain Muriel's abigail would not return, and his voice dropped to that of a whisper. "I expect to receive news of the search. I must remain until the messenger arrives."

"Oh!" Muriel immediately forgave him for his absence and silently apologized for her reckless judgment of his character. She simply could not be responsible for her actions at present. "Then why don't I stay with you? We can both travel to Almack's later together."

"Aunt Penny won't have it." Freddie wasn't going to tolerate the change of plans either. "If you don't go, she won't go. If she doesn't go, then Father won't bother to travel on his own, so we'll all be here when the messenger arrives, and we can't have that."

Of course he was right. Muriel, Aunt Penny, and Papa would just be in the way.

"Then you'll have *something* to tell me?" Relief spread through her. It had been an eternity since she'd learned of

Sherwin's disappearance. This was the first time she'd felt hopeful that some answer might be close at hand. "You promise?"

"I cannot guarantee that it's good news, but we shall know if our search efforts are in vain." Freddie took hold of Muriel by her shoulders. "Your task is the most difficult of all. It is an onerous role that requires the utmost bravery and courage."

Her task? So far Muriel had stood by and done nothing, nothing at all.

"You must be strong and maintain the belief that he will return," Freddie told her. "You must."

He was right. Muriel knew Freddie was right.

"If it is in Sherwin's power, if he is able . . . I know he will. I have no doubt. It is only . . ." She gazed up at her brother, losing her battle to restrain the tears that finally streaked down her cheeks when she spoke. "Oh, Freddie, what if he *cannot*?" She brought her hand to her lips and stifled her sob.

Chapter Fifteen

Muriel stepped into the assembly rooms at Almack's. All was as she had remembered—or, rather, what little she had remembered. She hadn't found any of her surroundings memorable in the least.

Off to one side stood her father, Aunt Penny, Mrs. Wilbanks, and Sir Samuel, all clearly in high humor. Muriel wished she could have shared in their cheer. At the moment she thought she'd never feel happy again. The best she could hope for was encouraging news about Sherwin, and she allowed that optimistic thought to sustain her.

"Lady Muriel!" Lady Amelia Whipple approached.

"Good evening, Lady Amelia." Muriel had to think of something to say to her to prevent the topic of Sherwin's disappearance surfacing. "Have you seen my cousin Constance? I cannot think she would miss the assembly."

"No, I am positive she is to attend." Lady Amelia nibbled on her lower lip. "I do not think she will be at all happy with the news I've just heard."

"What is it now?" Muriel had to admit she was mildly

curious and hoped this *on dit* had nothing to do with Sherwin. "What have you heard?"

"Sir Samuel Pruitt is engaged to be married."

"Engaged to whom?" Muriel was struck wide-eyed. Of course she had known he was about to offer for someone and had suspected it might have been her. Until now she hadn't taken the time to puzzle out who else he might have considered.

"I have no idea. She's stood up with him a number of times over this last week. I believe she's been out driving with him a time or two as well. And I collect he's sent her some very pretty flowers. Oh, Constance will be quite devastated when she learns of it! " Lady Amelia sniffed, appearing very sympathetic to Constance's plight. "The engagement has not been announced yet, but the news will crush her. She had resolutely set her cap for him after Lord Amhurst's elopement."

"We do not know that to be true," Muriel replied, maintaining that Sherwin's whispered-about race to Gretna Green had yet to be proven. Perhaps that was the news Freddie would receive tonight, a confirmation or denial of that piece of gossip.

"Why else would he have gone from Town so quickly?" Lady Amelia did not seem as though she would be easily convinced otherwise, and Muriel had no wish to try.

"I only caution you not to jump to conclusions. We know nothing of his circumstance. And we know nothing of Sir Samuel's." Muriel glanced back at her aunt and father. They still bubbled with far more joy and laughter than she'd seen in a very, very long time.

There was such cheer and animation. Something clearly had happened within their family circle. Certain that her father would not have accepted a marriage arrangement on her behalf, Muriel wondered if Lady Amelia had been mistaken. Perhaps Constance would not be crushed by the news of Sir Samuel's engagement because she was the lucky lady who had won his heart.

Sir Samuel had gone on about her just the other day. How excited he had become when he spoke her name. Could it be? Constance and Sir Samuel? Wouldn't that prove to be a strange turn of events if it were true?

The stupid notion was not easily banished from her thoughts. No, it simply could not be. Muriel refused to believe it.

Susan, who appeared absolutely radiant dangling off Sir Samuel's arm, approached Muriel and Lady Amelia.

"I thought you did not manage to acquire vouchers, Sukey." That is what Muriel remembered from last time, but her question was answered by observing the two of them together. "It's you! *You* and Sir Samuel are to be married!"

It was so very clear now. Susan was absolutely glowing with joy.

"I simply explained to the Patronesses that Miss Wilbanks is to be my bride, Lady Pruitt, before the end of the year." Sir Samuel glanced to Susan, who could not keep from smiling. "Lady Castlereagh issued a guest voucher and welcomed her at once."

Susan gazed at Sir Samuel with such affection, Muriel wondered how it was she could have missed noticing something so obvious before. But then, she had been so very preoccupied with her own secrets. This news, however, was simply wonderful.

"Miss Susan Wilbanks?" Lady Amelia uttered in stunned disbelief.

"It was all rather sudden, really," Susan went on to explain. "All these years I had always thought of him as kind and agreeable. I cannot know how or when our friendship turned into something more. It was all of a sudden . . . *different* between us, though I was afraid the same might not be true for him."

"It was," Sir Samuel assured his new fiancée. "I cannot believe that she'd been under my nose all this time, and I nearly did not notice her. I could not be happier."

Muriel felt as if she were fortunate as well. How wonderful it was that her two great friends had found each other. Sir Samuel, wed to Muriel's best friend, would, indeed, be part of the family.

"His Grace was kind enough to act as intermediary between me and Mr. Wilbanks, arranging the marriage settlement." Sir Samuel quickly returned to the topic of his future bride. "Will she not make the most perfect future duchess?"

Susan blushed at Sir Samuel's pronouncement, and Muriel could not have agreed more.

"The Earl of Brent to see you, Excellency." Giorgio stepped into Signore Biondi's small parlor where Sherwin sat and announced the visitor only moments before Freddie entered. He handed the footman the hat and gloves he'd just peeled off and tossed his greatcoat over the servant's arm.

"Where the devil have you been?" Freddie reached out to take hold of Sherwin's shoulders for a proper scolding but must have thought better of coming in too close. "I have people out looking for you, and Moo's worried sick."

Sherwin stood to properly greet his friend.

"Your note said you were in dire circumstances—" Apparently, upon setting eyes upon Sherwin, Freddie understood. "You look dreadful, ol' man. I had no idea. . . ."

"I'm sure it's not half as bad as I've been feeling these

last twenty-four hours." Sherwin still hadn't quite recovered. "I am sure I can relay all that has transpired at some later date, but I need to see Muriel. I need to find her, go to her at once. Where is she?"

Freddie eyed Sherwin. "Not looking like that, you won't. Even with her sturdy constitution, you'd give her a fright."

Sherwin glanced down at his attire. What remained of his once very fine clothing was ruined beyond repair.

"Moo's at Almack's—making a poor showing, if I might hazard a guess. She's hasn't been taking your absence well."

"I am sorry to cause her any distress." Sherwin could well imagine her frantic state of mind. It, most likely, was similar his own.

"Tell me it's not true what they're saying about you making a dash for Gretna Green with some milk-and-water miss." Freddie, it seemed, needed to know this small detail.

"No, I daresay, I did not." Sherwin did not wish to delve into just how close he had come to matrimony. "Does Muriel believe the same? I must assure her my affection for her has not altered in the least."

"You won't make it past Lady Jersey, ol' man," Freddie intoned with disapproval. "Any of the Almack's Patronesses will block your entry if you're dressed like that. You'll need knee breeches—can't show up in trousers, no matter how fine they're cut." He snapped his fingers. "It occurs to me that Weston's got your measurements. Mayhap he can manage to put together a getup for you."

"He may have some of the clothing I've ordered on hand." Sherwin knew his departure from Town had been made in haste, and his purchases might well lie at the tailor shop undelivered.

"That's the spirit!" Freddie cheered. "I'll dispatch a note and have Weston send over a set of evening clothes."

"At this hour?" Sherwin reeled at Freddie's audacity of summoning a shopkeeper as if on a whim. "He's bound to have closed his shop by now."

"He'd jolly well better come if he knows what's good for him." Freddie did not sound as if he were joking.

"There's paper, ink, and a quill over there." Sherwin gestured toward the writing desk Signore Biondi had used earlier.

"How much time do we have? What hour is it?" Freddie pulled up a chair and set to work.

"I have no idea; I had to trade my pocket watch for passage on the mail coach." Sherwin turned about, squinting in his search for a mantel clock, which, at this distance, he could read. "Nearly eight."

"We need to hurry." Freddie handed the note to Giorgio, who alerted Marcello to make the delivery. "I've just had another thought." Taking up the quill, he motioned in the air before penning a second missive. "I'll send for Sturgis, my father's valet. We'll need his talent along with a supply of starched linens to—" He wriggled his fingers in the general area of his throat. "Just in case, you know. Bound to have problems there."

Apparently Lewis was not the only valet who struggled with the crafting of cravats.

"I think we'll have him bring a quizzing glass for you— it'll help you see, won't it?" Freddie lifted his head, waiting for Sherwin's response.

"Somewhat." Sherwin vowed that he would not be without one, even when he wore his spectacles.

"Good." With the second correspondence dried, folded, and sealed, Freddie handed it to Giorgio for delivery. "You'll need to bathe before either one of them arrives," he told Sherwin, "You're wearing an entire day's travel."

Sherwin glanced down at himself. He had to agree, he was filthy. Muriel might not care about his appearance, but he felt quite certain her family would. He had to remember, he had not yet gained permission from His Grace to wed his daughter.

"All right, off you go, then." Freddie waved him away. "I expect you've got vouchers to Almack's, right? Hate to go through this exercise only to find you won't be welcome at the front door."

Taking the stairs up to the first floor, Sherwin felt more nervous attending Almack's this evening than he had at the opening night last week. He stopped midway up the staircase and stared at the Hessians on his feet. "Wait a moment—can't wear these in. What am I to do?"

"If you hadn't insisted we dash off the instant Sturgis had his back turned, before he'd finished giving you a polish," Freddie scolded, "you wouldn't be asking!"

"He was taking forever." Sherwin, who had been appreciative of his friend and his father's valet, could not help but complain. "We'd never have left the house if we hadn't bolted."

"Sturgis never would have missed this. Been given the sack if he had, I daresay." Freddie paused only long enough to size up their situation and replied, "Look here, ol' man. We've about the same size feet, what? Take mine." He kicked off his black dancing slippers, abandoning them.

Sherwin reached downward to grab hold of his left boot, but the tight fit of his jacket held him immobile.

"That's no good. You'll never be able to manage." Standing in his stocking feet, Freddie latched on to the toe and heel of one Hessian and pulled while Sherwin held on to the handrail.

After a few sizeable yanks, it came off. Freddie dropped

it to the floor, and it landed with a muffled thud. He went to work on the right boot, which came off with the same amount of effort, and it was deposited near the first in short order.

With a fluid motion, Sherwin easily slid into the dress slippers and made to continue on his way up the staircase.

With a hand to Sherwin's arm, Freddie slowed their progress. He had already pushed his foot into the first boot and then stepped into the other, hopping his way precariously up the staircase after Sherwin.

"Hold on—the blasted things are a bit snugger than I expected." He reached down to adjust them on his feet and nearly tipped over. "What time is it now?"

"Sorry." Sherwin didn't know what he could do about the Earl's discomfort now, but if they did not hurry, neither one would be allowed to enter. "I haven't a—"

Freddie glanced down at the watch he'd extracted from his vest pocket. "Zounds—it's dashed near eleven. We'd best get a move on. They close the doors then, don't you know?" He kept a firm hold of Sherwin, preventing him from moving forward. "I'll be barred from admittance in any case in these cursed boots. Look here, I'll create a diversion. When they go for me, you slip in on the side, got that? You keep a careful lookout."

Sherwin didn't know how he'd manage to bypass the Patronesses without being seen, but he'd have to give it a go.

Freddie waved him to the side, and Sherwin flattened himself against the wall, inching his way toward the front portal, being mindful not to be seen.

Not merely marching but strutting with definite purpose toward the entrance, Freddie bid the sentry a hearty "Hallo." The steward motioned for the footman, in turn, to detain the tardy guest and summon one of the Patronesses to deal with the dress code infraction.

"Oh, come now, do be a good fellow and allow me to sit while I wait. These things fit most abominably." Freddie grimaced, making a great fuss over the boots.

The footman acquiesced, and Freddie sat against the wall, where he was watched most carefully by the second footman attending the portal.

"My Lord Brent." Lady Jersey approached the Earl. "I simply cannot believe this. I know you are well aware that Hessians are forbidden."

"No matter, Sally," Mrs. Drummond-Burrell intoned, joining their gathering. "It is past eleven. He cannot enter."

"*Past* eleven? Only just." Freddie made a big show of flourishing his pocket watch, doing what he could to attract as much attention as he could, and with his other hand he waved for Sherwin to make his move.

Sherwin slipped in unnoticed, clearing the first obstacle. He moved past the crimson ropes that separated the entry area from the dancers; now all he need do was locate Muriel somewhere within. Never had his long-sightedness served him so well. Sherwin worked his way from the right side of the first room to the left side, moving from familiar face to unknown face until such time as he would positively identify his—

There she was, looking a veritable angel dressed all in white. So very beautiful. All the effort, hardship, and difficulties he had endured trudging to London—seeing her now was worth every effort he had made. Muriel. He felt like shouting, crowing, singing! It was all he could do not to call out to her.

He had to remain calm. Sherwin moved through the guests, and on his way toward her he could hear a chorus of "Amhurst"s whispered in his wake.

He did not care who gossiped about him or what they

said. By the end of this evening his name and Muriel's would be permanently linked, and everyone could talk about them all they liked.

Sherwin stopped some distance away from her. The guests around him ebbed, leaving him and Muriel standing to one side of the room.

A sudden quiet surrounded her, and Muriel glanced around to discern the reason. A man stood at the end of the room.

Muriel thought she saw Sherwin.

She blinked. Perhaps she was dreaming. The guests around her seemed to have dissolved, leaving only him standing there alone. At least, it looked like him.

"Sherwin . . . ," she whispered. She wanted to run into his arms, but her lower limbs refused to obey. She stood there, unable to move, her eyes filled with tears at the joy of seeing him after so long, after so much worrying. Here he was, safe and near.

At that moment she had no care as to where he had been or how he had come to return to her side. All Muriel cared about was that he was there now. Explanations of his absence would, no doubt, follow in due time.

He stepped toward her at an unimaginably slow pace. Why did he not run? Take her in his arms, as she wanted him to do? Did he not know she had been struck immobile?

"Lady Muriel." His voice cracked in an achingly familiar, emotion-filled tremor.

"Sherwin," Muriel repeated. He had returned, just as she had known he would if he could.

A familiar musical interlude announced that the waltz would begin soon.

"Our dance, I think." He offered her his arm, and she had never been so happy to accept his escort.

She laid her hand upon his sleeve. He was real, proving she hadn't imagined his presence.

"I am sorry for the anguish I have inflicted upon you." He stood by her side, ready to perform the promenade. His warm, comforting hand covered hers.

"I am certain it was not of your doing." Muriel arched her arm over her head and gazed into his wonderfully brown eyes.

"No, it wasn't," he whispered, gazing into hers. "All I wanted was to return to Town, to find you once more. I promise you, we *will* be married."

"To hold you close for this dance will suffice for now." Muriel stepped around him in time to the music, delighting in his proximity.

"I vow that nothing, no one, will ever separate us again." Sherwin brought his hand to her waist, while she rested her hands upon his shoulders. "You see, my dear, it is true, *amore vincit omnia*."

Muriel smiled up at him, again stared into his eyes, and allowed a small, throaty giggle to escape.

Love did, indeed, conquer all.

10/13 em